URSOCRYPHA

The Book of Bear

KATIE WELCH

Cover and illustration by Dylan Stinson

ISBN: 1539516660
ISBN 13: 9781539516668

to Will Stinson
with love

ACKNOWLEDGEMENTS

Thank you to word-creator Suzanne M. Steele for the title, and for her guidance, wisdom and friendship; Patricia Dupuis, though we didn't work together on this particular book, I am profoundly grateful for your brilliant and heartfelt editorial counsel; thanks to Mary Woodbury, for seeing the strengths in The Bears *and thus inspiring* Ursocrypha; *and for their encouragement and faith thank you to Kim Collier, Norah Ashmore, Kathleen Jones, Judy Petersen and Shauna Tsuchiya.*

Thanks to my daughters, Olivia and Heather Hughes, for their unwavering love and support. Special thanks to Thomas A. Brown, teacher and friend. Tom, you nurtured and informed a love for nature and the outdoors in me thirty years ago. You are the original inspiration for this book; may the Great Bear bless you. Dylan Stinson, for your fabulous artwork, insight, and vision, thank you! Thanks to my project team at CreateSpace. Gratitude and thanks to the great teachers and friends who have put their faith in me. Your confidence in my abilities has sustained me through the years: Donna & Paul Bishop, Quinn Collier, Fred Flahiff, Norman Handy, J. Douglass Hume, Sidney Katz, Elizabeth McCullough, Shelly McKerchar,

Sheldon Shore, Julie Threinen. Thank you also to my family, especially my brother Tim and sister Maureen, who have always encouraged me to write.

Thank you to everyone working to protect nature and wilderness around the world and especially in northern British Columbia.

I have dedicated this book to Will Stinson, but his name needs to be here as well because without his love, help, faith, encouragement, and support, Ursocrypha *would still be in my head and not in your hands.*

Preface to Ursocrypha: The Book of Bear, *formerly* The Bears

At a time of great upheaval in my personal life, when the Pacific Northwest coast of British Columbia was under direct and imminent environmental threat, I decided to do something I had always wanted to do: write a book. Impatient to hold a physical book that I had written, after a cursory, impersonal editorial process, I self-published The Bears *in December, 2012. In spite of rushing to publish* The Bears, *and doing the bare minimum of marketing with limited distribution channels, the book gathered a small but enthusiastic audience.*

Other writing projects followed The Bears. *I completed a young adult adventure manuscript, and another work of adult fiction. I hired a phenomenal editor who taught and is still teaching me a great deal about the craft of writing. I met other writers, attended a writer's circle, and studied the bones of writing.*

In the summer of 2016 I was invited to read from The Bears *at WORD Vancouver, a festival of writing in all forms, promoting literacy and reading. I hadn't picked up a copy of* The Bears *and examined it since the year it was published. When I read my own book, I recognized the story, but it was as though a stranger had written it. I revised the manuscript. The title had always been problematic – everyone thought it was a children's book. Friend and poet Suzanne M. Steele fused some title ideas I had into* Ursocrypha: The Book of Bear.

I send this story back out into the world, and hope it makes more friends.

Katie Welch

"Who trusted God was love indeed
And love Creation's final law
Tho' Nature, red in tooth and claw
With ravine, shriek'd against his creed"

—*In Memoriam A.H.H., Canto 56*
Alfred, Lord Tennyson

URSOCRYPHA: THE BOOK OF BEAR

THE GREAT BEAR CREATES THE WORLD

In the beginning there was only the Great Bear. Everything was dark, because when the Great Bear opened her eyes, her head was tucked into her own belly. She saw only the blackness of her own fur. Then the Great Bear knew herself, and she knew she was alone. Keeping her head tucked into her black-furred belly, she licked and licked until her fur lay flat in one spot. She extended one long, sharp claw and drew it across this place. Little beads of blood formed in a line, and fell down in drops, and became the Black Bears of the earth.

The Great Bear unfolded herself, and stood over her Black Bears. She realized that she had to move her bowels and she did so, squatting on her rear haunches and releasing little pellets. These fell down and became the Brown Bears of the earth.

The Great Bear breathed in, and with this intake of breath she created the wind. She exhaled, and the moisture from her breath created the rain. Then the Great Bear blinked and peered out onto the horizon, and this created light—a great, blinding flash of pure white light. The Great

Bear's eyes watered, and her tears fell down, and they became the White Bears of the earth. Because they did not fall under the Great Bear's body they were not warm, and the place where the White Bears fell was white and cold and frozen.

The Great Bear surveyed her creations, the Black, White, and Brown Bears, and she was pleased. She saw wind ruffle their fur and rain slake their thirst. She saw her bears had no home, and in that moment she felt that she was about to give birth to a cub. The Great Bear delivered her child, which she named Earth. If you look up in the night sky, you will see Ursa Major, the mother of us all, and Ursa Minor, our mother's cub, which is also our home.

Gently, the Great Bear took the Black Bears of the earth in her mouth and put them on her cub's back. Then she carefully placed the Brown Bears of the earth on her cub's stomach. She took the White Bears of the earth, and their frozen home, and she put all of this on her cub's tail. The Great Bear saw that all of her bears moved comfortably on the surface of her cub.

She sent her cub to walk among the stars.

Tlingit

Hungry. I am ravenous. I think about my own teeth scraping my insides, my bleeding insides, eating blood, so hungry I eat my own insides. Sharp yellow teeth itching for crunch and suck of seal bone. Edges of whiteness are seeping red. Where can Tlingit find seal—sweet, sweet seal meat? Think of the first claw ripping open soft fur. Think of jelly fat inside mouth and inside throat, moving fast past teeth sore from seal skull crushing.

Slowly moving, moving slowly, over brown-grey-not-white. Where once was white of snow, now only brown of rock. Brown-grey-not-white holds nothing, strange hot sharp rock, strange lack of white. Whiteness should be seeping red. High sun hot why? Sun high and hot. I return, turn and re-turn, to find big cold empty water with maybe fish, maybe seal. Seal swimming faster, slipping away, nowhere to hide on cold hard ice, nowhere to hide and kill.

Hungry I am, ravenous.

MOKSGM'OL

The river has been generous this warm time. Another long, strong fish flails in my jaws – there must be thirty like it in my belly—belly full of fat pink flesh. I release this fish to smooth round stones. It arches, silver red scales flashing, slit eyes bulging in the air. I let it thrash. Scales shred on rocks, rips and tears split its tail.

The fish buckles, flips and flops down to the river. This Fish Spirit wants to join the clear, winking river once again. Not permissible, for am I not Moksgm'ol?

Moksgm'ol of the forest, announcing my presence with creamy white fur flashes through green after green, bough upon bough, moss and rock, rain and branch, sun and wind! Moksgm'ol who eats—nay, feasts—at my leisure and my pleasure! Moksgm'ol, Keeper of Dreams, Keeper of Memory! Moksgm'ol who reigns, shining white crown, stalking unhindered throughout my Great Rainforest Kingdom!

YUKUAI (HAPPY)

First I smelled the bamboo—so much fresh bamboo, crisp green sugar smells, so many—and through the grasses I pushed toward the smells-which-mean-delicious. Now I remember another smell too, some strange, sick perfume.

Ling Ling was behind me, I felt her there, but the bamboo smelled so good. Later, I learned that Pyung, En Lai, and Chiu Chiu were also nearby, lured by the fresh food smells, and captured in the same way I was.

When the oh-so-sweet bamboo was close, the grasses were close also—too close, I think now—a tunnel of bamboo and grasses made by the deathmen, leading into a hard, black-barred-box. Later, when all of the green grasses browned and the bamboo died and fell away, I saw I was in a black-barred-box. The fresh bamboo had been placed inside these boxes to trick us.

Juicy flesh of bamboo squirting under my teeth—I ate three, four bites before the stink and sound of the deathmen came. An ugly gong sound clanged, and then the grasses and bamboo would not move. I pushed with limbs, bit with jaws, ripped with claws. The grasses had stiff, immovable parts that did not yield to bite or slash. These were the black bars of the box.

Once, I believed that Good Fortune was with me that day. She compelled my stomach and urged me to gorge on the bamboo. I saw nothing of the deathmen until I was properly snared beyond escape.

Once, I believed En Lai was frowned upon by Good Fortune that day. He turned before the black bars closed behind him, and the deathmen smote him with long sticks. Perhaps this hurt. I don't remember hearing En Lai call out in pain. His moans came later, when the grasses had died, and I saw him lying on his side in a black box like mine.

Now I know better. Good Fortune smiled on En Lai. Good Fortune opened her gold-stitched red robes, smiled her small, enigmatic smile, and released the deathmen with their sticks to slash at his belly. He died quickly; he never knew all the black-barred-boxes of the Great Wide World, or the legions of white-faced deathmen outside of them, looking in.

The Great Bear Creates People

It was summer, and the Brown Bears of the earth were too warm. The cubs began to cry because they were so hot, and they begged their mothers to cool them down. The mothers taught their cubs to cool off in water, and to lie in the shade of leafy green trees. It was no use, though—nothing cooled the cubs enough, and they cried and cried.

The Great Bear heard the incessant crying of the cubs and took pity on them. She reached down and licked them with her great tongue to cool them off. But when the Great Bear licked the Brown Bear cubs, all of their fur came off, and they were naked. The cubs were happy then, and they ran here and there, their pale skin growing pink and then red under the intense sun. Soon, they had painful sunburns, and they began to cry again in earnest.

The Brown Bear mothers heard their cubs crying and went to find them. When the bear mothers saw these pinkish red creatures, they did not recognize their own children. The cubs' crying had attracted predators. Wolf was there, and Coyote. Cougar lurked nearby. Overhead, Eagle circled, anticipating a feast.

The Great Bear saw the naked cubs would be eaten if she didn't intervene. She had to act quickly to save their lives. She pulled the cubs up onto their hind legs, took away their tails, and gave them the gift of intelligence, so they could escape from their enemies. With the blessing of intelligence came the curse of self-consciousness, and the cubs, realizing they were naked, grew ashamed. They ran and hid themselves in the bushes.

That's right, run and hide, little naked ones, said the Great Bear. *Be cunning, and do not show yourselves. Walk lightly and quietly on the earth so that your enemies will not hear you. Use the abundance of the earth to feed yourselves, to stay warm in the winter, and to house yourselves and your young.*

The constellation Boötes, wide at the shoulders and narrow at the feet, stands upright to represent People in the heavens.

MOKSGM'OL

I, the mighty Moksgm'ol, move lazily toward the fish I do not want to eat. Its thrashes are still powerful, but my jaws will close around its silver sides and end its life. Then there is movement upriver—a rippling presence in the thick tall cedars. I turn from the fish, raise my head, and flare my nostrils. Who dares interrupt Moksgm'ol mid-feed?

I do not discover who dares. The pierce of Eagle's shriek blasts from over my head. I turn back in time to see Eagle's perfect arc, and the spread of his vast wings as he swoops down from a tall treetop. His talons penetrate the fish—my fish, the fish of Moksgm'ol—at the nadir of his dive. He then soars to the zenith of a new green perch far above me.

I release my jaw and roar my complaint. But Eagle knows he has deceived me. He settles on a cedar snag within my sight and begins to eat my fish with impudence, high above me. He tears at the pink flesh with his savage yellow beak, and raises his white head to gulp the meat down his gullet.

I turn my creamy backside to Eagle and walk away slowly, my paws squishing in the carcasses of my salmon kills. Moksgm'ol has plenty, and will catch plenty more. The riverbanks are rank and red with the remains of my meals.

KITIMAT

Before disaster struck, he felt it coming, but was powerless to stop it. He was ambushed, arms tied behind his back, tensed up, prepared for a punch.

Gilbert Crow woke up four times that night, the worst night since the project had passed. The Black Snake now undulated through the forest. Formal talks, negotiations, protests, news reports, public outcry—all were futile. Big money won. Poison was pulled from the earth, sucked from the depths where it safely lay. Land and forest were rent asunder, allowing the Black Snake to wind its way to the Great Water. Viscous black blood was sent by pipeline and then tanker to people who hungered for easy fuel.

In pale dawn light, Gilbert slipped into jeans, a flannel shirt, and wool socks. Fifty-two degrees latitude: September was less autumn, more early winter, the morning air like cold hands slapping his brown cheeks.

He shuffled across the wooden floor, filled a heavy black kettle, and slid it noisily onto the cast-iron top of the wood stove. Smoke sighed out of the front of the stove as he opened it, and the hinges squeaked. Orange embers were still dancing inside. He added a little more wood and a few more sticks of fuel—the bare minimum required for boiling water. He mumbled his gratitude to the Creator, giving thanks for this fuel, this heat, this source of life and living.

There were dirty forms of energy, and clean forms. The clean ones were simple, and the Creator offered them freely. The sun offered warmth, and its orange rays beamed down. Opening soft green arms, the great cedars of the forest flourished and thrived by capturing the sun's energy. The great lips of the Creator blew steady winds, and wise Eagle used these to his advantage, fuelling movement under his brown and white wings. Ocean tides surged in and out, kinetic energy, freely given.

The wood burning in his stove, little flames licking at its sides, was a hundred-year-old tree, struck down for the power inside of her. This grand old lady of the forest shed grey, sooty robes of ash, the dirty clothes of time-accrued energy, dirtier than the sun's warm hands, or the wind's fresh breath. Wood ash was dirty, but not as filthy as the blood of the Black Snake.

After a breakfast of fish and buttered toast, Gilbert walked to the riverbank. He shut his front door cautiously, unwilling to mar the hush of morning with a boorish slam. He stretched on his front porch, long arms reaching so high his fingers grazed the ceiling, straight chestnut hair falling evenly to his waist. He often wore his hair in a single braid, but today he was eager to walk, so he tied it impatiently into a loose ponytail.

With two big strides, Gilbert descended four wooden steps, and set off on his accustomed river-bound trail through the forest. He walked at a quicker-than-usual, anxious pace, edgy with sleeplessness, worried about how much worse off the forest would be since the construction of the pipeline. Sunlight filtered through swooping cedar branches, reflected in drops of dew lining fern fronds.

An accidental rupture of the Black Snake, a spill of its blood, and the fragile, unique ecology of the coastal temperate rainforest would be irreparably damaged. Birds would be rendered flightless, slick black chemical sludge encasing their feathers. Fish would be choked with foreign poisons. Some of them would die immediately, while others would carry smaller—though still deadly—quantities of black goo within them, for the Spirit bear to consume in increments. Although he was at the top of the food chain, Moksgm'ol, the Spirit bear, would die the most insidious death. Some chemical-induced cancer would eat away his unique biology from the inside.

Gilbert and the Haisla people had argued, researched, and referenced ancient knowledge to stop the snake from coming. The cumulative intelligence remained, dancing incessantly in Gilbert's thoughts. No wonder he couldn't sleep. He wasn't alone in his terror-induced insomnia. His friends Gary and Sandra confessed to waking in cold sweats from nightmares – black sludge oozing in the forest, pooling in the ocean.

This golden fall morning shouldn't be poignant, Gilbert thought bitterly. Clean smell of giant red cedars, rain evaporating from billions of Sitka spruce needles, undertones of moss, of worms at work in rotting vegetation, and the tang of salty ocean all became secondary to the pungency of decaying fish as Gilbert approached the Kitimat River. Salmon had returned to spawn in record numbers this year, in spite of the recently completed industrial dockyard blocking the river's mouth. The fish were here to spawn, to create life and then die. Behind the salmon, ships came to carry cargos of slow death across the ocean.

The shady darkness of surrounding trees receded as the narrow walking trail opened up along the riverbank. Gilbert felt a tingling sensation, a presence, so he hung back among the trees to observe. Clear water gurgled and sloshed over the smooth stones. Insects buzzed and chirped. Birds rustled and called, adding solo flourishes to the water's chorus.

He saw a flash of creamy fur. Downstream, maybe forty meters away – Moksgm'ol, the Spirit bear! He hadn't appeared this close to Kitimat since before the Black Snake! Gilbert held his breath. The bear was a good-sized one, a male he guessed, probably close to three hundred pounds.

Moksgm'ol slapped at an injured salmon. The fish writhed and flopped under his great muddy paws. Dozens of other salmon were scattered along the shore in various stages of death and decay.

Gilbert felt giddy with relief. He was often sleepless when Moksgm'ol was nearby. His terrible fears of impending disaster and doom were perhaps just that—fears, and nothing more. He watched the Spirit bear, and a smooth, round river stone dropped into the pond of his soul. His body remained motionless, but his spirit expanded, ripples passing outward in waves that moved in every direction, three dimensionally, to the compass points and also up into the air toward the blue, white, and grey sky, and down into the earth beneath him. The worm beneath Gilbert's feet felt Gilbert's soul expand, and expanded each of its segments, pushing little clods of dirt and tiny stones into new air pockets. A beetle scuttled up a green twig and waved her antennae around, the better to receive vibrations. The Sitka spruce, the red cedar, the western hemlock, and the Douglas fir whispered their pleasure, smooth susurration of needles brushing against each other.

Eagle felt Gilbert's joy and snapped his head around sharply, yellow eyes boring into Moksgm'ol's broad backside. *O Moksgm'ol, you greedy-guts,* thought the eagle. *I'll teach you not to play with your food.* Eagle shrugged his powerful shoulders, made himself into an arrow, and dove from his perch, shrieking with delight, crooking claws to snag the Spirit bear's still-flailing fish.

TLINGIT

Big, cold, empty water. Water is wanting. Water wants its winter clothes of icy blue and white. Water is naked. Swim in water. Move slowly again slowly again slowly—rhythm of swimming paws pressing patterns into big cold empty water. When water is naked, swimming is long. Magic seals melted icy blue water clothes, then disappeared in big cold empty water? The water has no edges, and the space has no limits—no seals, no fish. Hungry I am.

Water edges there must be. Inside ribs scraping empty bloody guts. Tasting blood—blood from ravenous stomach tasting. Always seeing white at edge of water meeting sky. Move through water—emptier, colder. White edges stay far away always, white edges never move close. Now the sun comes lower and more, and pushes winter away.

Think about K'ytuk. Don't think about K'ytuk. Please, please forget little K'ytuk—the feel of K'ytuk inside me, below hungry belly, moving inside me below my hungry belly. Belly pains crunched my insides all day and then tiny, bloody K'ytuk outside my body. Lick blood from K'ytuk—lick and taste my body's blood from new fur of my baby.

No think K'ytuk—heart hurting to think baby K'ytuk lost into warm waters not swimming, not breathing. Think anything, something, anything, to not remember how there was no end to the water and how K'ytuk could not...think not...think of the old stories. Think something other—not pain, not water, not nothing-where-there-used-to-be-ice.

Churchill Northern Studies Centre, Churchill, Manitoba

None of it helped: the numbers, the statistics, the ratios, the research, the documentation, the photographs, the videos, the reports. None of it was helping, and her sense of futility was growing, along with her anger.

When she had applied to do her post-graduate research at the Northern Studies Centre in Churchill, Anne McCraig had fondly imagined herself striding over the subarctic, achieving a fitness level unprecedented in her thirty-five years of life. She had pictured a transformation. She had started as a pretty, chubby blonde girl who loved animals, then morphed into a pretty-but-round teenager, widely admired for her brains, but chosen last for every team sport in gym. The teenager emerged from her adolescent chrysalis as a fatter caterpillar, a hopeless undergraduate endomorph, alleviating the stress of final exams with litres of cookie dough ice cream and greasy grilled-cheese sandwiches liberally dipped in ketchup. *When I get out in the field,* Anne thought, *all this will change. Outside doing actual research, moving my body.* The world would at last see the intrepid Anne McCraig, the one who had been pupating, waiting for her moment to arrive. Prior to her departure for Manitoba, Anne had even purchased—she blushed to think of it now—an outfit in a size smaller than what she usually wore.

Wapusk National Park wasn't the weight loss program Anne had hoped it would be. She had been toiling in this remote shoreline community for over a year now, and she was in worse shape than when she had arrived. Collecting data in the field was such a small part of the work. The majority of her labour involved sitting in front of a computer with a tray of date squares and a pot of sweet tea at her dimpled elbow. In any event, she and her only potential romantic interest at the centre, Ian Findlay, had mutually decided to be nothing more than friends.

Ian Findlay had a good-natured approach to work and life. Tall and gangling, he was clumsy, and had a goofy laugh that belied his professional competence. Thirty-three years old and unmarried, he was utterly devoted to the study of botany. Each of his romantic entanglements resembled the others, he told Anne. Each began with an initial lighthearted courtship and the discovery of common interests, followed by an intermediate time of increasing awkwardness, as the compass needle of his attention swung back to the magnetic zero of his scientific interests and curiosity. Last came an endgame of unreturned phone calls, and bored sighs over listless dinners.

Anne and Ian knew each other's histories because of sporadic boozy late nights at the research centre. Jane retired early, inevitably. Then Ian and Anne compared awkward date stories until the boisterous hilarity roused Jane, and she appeared, glowering, demanding they shut up and go to bed.

Then came the heartbreak of Tlingit. Tlingit had emerged thin but victorious from her den early the previous spring. Polar bears often had two cubs in a litter, but Tlingit had emerged that spring with a single cub. He—a male, the biologists quickly determined—was the youngest, smallest polar bear cub that Anne had ever seen, and the first she had laid eyes on outside captivity. He was pure white, a puffball, with round imploring eyes. For Anne, he represented love, surrogate motherhood, and professional curiosity, bundled up with her hopes, fears, and dreams.

"Let's call him K'ytuk!" she gushed.

"Don't make an emotional investment," Jane said.

"You *do* need to maintain professional distance," Ian counselled.

Damn them both, Anne thought, and proceeded to order photographic enlargements of Tlingit's precious offspring. She pinned them up in the common room, her office, her bedroom. She fretted about K'ytuk's welfare, while her logical, scientific mind recorded facts pointing to what an increasingly inhospitable environment the north was becoming for polar bears.

It happened early one day in June. Anne woke early, surprised by the sound of the howling wind. She lay in bed watching the erratic gusts of an unseasonable blizzard toss snow back and forth outside of her window. Anne knew Tlingit was out there, hungry herself and frantic to feed K'ytuk. Mid-morning, Anne and Ian ventured out to the Hudson Bay shoreline. The wind and snow were severe. They wore enormous down parkas with faux-fur-trimmed hoods, and ski goggles to protect their eyes. It was a bad day for fieldwork. Anne suspected Ian of tagging along out of sympathy.

Squinting through the snow, they saw Hudson Bay was wild. Enormous steel-grey waves tossed and heaved. Adult bears could easily drown out there; cubs wouldn't stand a chance. *I hope they are on land right now*, Anne thought. At last the snow and wind retreated. Dark clouds separated, revealing patches of pale sky.

Ian spotted her first. She was standing right at the shoreline, swaying, sniffing, and searching, her muzzle pointed out over the water. She was alone. Anne made a small choking sound. She grasped Ian's forearm and squeezed it in distress. Then Tlingit began to vocalize. Long, desolate moans issued from her great, black-rimmed mouth. The polar bear tilted her head back and bawled.

Ian pushed Anne's hand away and scrambled to pull his video camera from its shoulder pouch. Tlingit continued to alternately sniff out over Hudson Bay, then toss her head back and moan. It was a heart-wrenching sound—an uncannily human sound of grief. Ian recorded her for seven minutes, then steered the silently weeping Anne back to the research centre, her open mouth mutely mirroring the mourning bear.

"It's a unique recording," Jane admitted, sitting at her desk, watching the little image on Ian's camera, and listening to the strange sounds emanating from the mother bear. "Polar bears aren't vocalizers. Except for when they are growling in a play fight, chuffing in anger, or mating, they don't make noise. I've never heard of it. But you don't know it's grief."

"What do your instincts tell you?" snapped Anne through her tears.

Now Anne sat in the CNSC library, shuffling her index cards and drinking herbal tea, afflicted with the torpor that plagued her since Tlingit had returned without her cub. Ian Findlay and Jane Minoto—*Doctor* Jane Minoto, Anne mentally corrected herself—were capable of detaching and academically appraising the situation. Anne mentally capitalized it: the Situation, in which the animals she had devoted her life to studying were starving and dying.

Anne closed her eyes, remembering Tlingit's moans as the mother bear stood on the shores of Hudson Bay, bereft.

"All we're doing is documenting their demise!" Anne had coughed through her tears.

"We are making a significant contribution to the scientific community, regardless of the bears' fate," Jane had answered, blinking, dry-eyed.

"Contributions as what?" Anne had wailed. "Historians?"

"Drama won't help," Jane had intoned. "In any case, you don't know what happened to Tlingit's cub. You're drawing conclusions without any evidence to support them."

"*Evidence?* What more evidence do you need? There's thirty-five percent less ice this year than there was last year, they were starving when they left, and the cub was too weak to walk on its own. Tlingit was *desperate*."

"Once again, you anthropomorphize and project," Jane had answered. *Smarmy,* Anne had thought, *condescending*. "This planet has been through huge temperature fluctuations in its long history. Your myopia is interfering with your objectivity."

I'd rather be shortsighted and have a heart, than be a dispassionate little smudge like her, Anne thought, her mind snapping back to the present.

Dr. Jane Minoto was slight and tidy. Anne slumped even lower in her seat, jealous of the senior scientist's small, muscular body. Anne's curves were always threatening to become rolls of—let's face it—fat.

Four months had elapsed since Ian had made the recording. Since then, Anne had watched and listened to the seven-minute clip hundreds of times. She had slowed it down, sped it up, and compared it with every other recorded polar bear vocalization that she could find. She sat at her computer, watching, listening, grieving, and eating. She was consuming calories while Tlingit was unable to. She was growing wider, while the bear was growing narrower.

The Great Bear Creates Pandas

At one time, all of the bears lived in peace on their part of Small Bear—the earth—ignorant of each other's existence. The White Bears of the earth lived far out in the cold of Small Bear's tail, the Brown Bears of the earth lived on Small Bear's warm tummy, and the Black Bears of the earth stayed on Small Bear's back.

Then came an exceptionally cold year, and the White Bears strayed farther down Small Bear's back than they ever had before in search of food. They wandered so far that they eventually strayed into the territory of the Black Bears. The Black Bears did not see the White Bears at first, as the Black Bears were hibernating and staying close to their dens. But Snake stirred early that year, and one morning, while warming his blood in the sun, Snake saw a White Bear for the first time.

Snake had grown bored after the long winter, so he decided to make some trouble. He slithered to the Black Bears' den and hissed that he had seen a bear bigger and much more beautiful than them. He hissed that he had seen a pure *white* bear. The Black Bears were incredulous at first, but their natural curiosity overtook them, and eventually they followed

Snake to a rocky place where the White Bears were harvesting berries from shrubs growing there.

The Black Bears growled and roared in anger when they saw their food supply being diminished by these intruders. Then the White Bears, whose stomachs were shrunken with hunger, growled and roared back. The Black Bears and the White Bears began fighting each other. Soon the rocky place was a blur of black fur and white fur as the bears grievously injured each other.

The Great Bear heard the commotion of the battle below. She bent her head down to the place on her cub where the battle was taking place, and she separated the White and Black Bears with her tongue, but one of each kind got caught between her teeth. The Great Bear then chewed and spat them out. When she looked down, she saw that she had made a new kind of bear that was both black and white, and that was the bear that we call Panda Bear. The Great Bear sent them to live on Small Bear's chest.

If you look up in the night sky, you can see Snake, the constellation also known as Draco, and Panda, which is also called Cepheus.

YUKUAI

The bamboo fields of my homeland seem a dream to me now. Perhaps I am dreaming them. I imagine them as a kind of Heaven—a green, waving land of plenty, a fresh water place of food everywhere and always, as far as one can roam. The roaming itself is paradise, lumbering wherever one wishes without impediment. Are these dreams or memories? If I could, I would ask Pyung or Ling Ling, because they were part of the dream. It seems to me that they were there in the endless fields of bamboo. Pyung or Ling Ling, if they live, must be living some life similar to this one I am living now—this infinitesimal, limited life.

On cold black starry nights, I remember warm bodies like mine around me—an expanse of black and white fur. Here in this prison, I am surrounded only by air, damp with rain, or frigid with frost and snow. I shiver.

Some nights the cold bites. It is almost intolerable. On nights like these, I remember Die Nacht der Feuers, the Firenight. I remember the screams of a hundred animals, inescapable heat, machines of the deathmen roaring overhead. I remember the very foam of fear evaporating from my bared teeth and lips— flames shooting upward everywhere, clouds of smoke burning my throat and eyes. I remember the Firenight, and although I am cold, the mere memory of burning warms my skin and fur, and I sleep.

Cologne, Germany, February 1939

"You instructed me to purchase a lucrative attraction. The bear is healthy, and there are no other bears like it in Germany at present. I secured the panda at your behest. Do with the creature what you wish, I will have my compensation," Lothar transferred the heavy black telephone to his left shoulder.

Greta entered her husband's office, balancing a tea tray on the broad shelf of her breasts. Her face was inexpressive as she approached a mammoth desk and deposited the tray with a clatter in front of her husband's polished black boots, left crossed over right on top of the brown leather blotter.

"*Quiet*," Lothar hissed. Then he yelled into the telephone, "Nein, not you, Herr Gunn! My wife – she constantly interrupts –" Lothar swung his legs up, leather boots narrowly missing the lunch, a grey boiled egg and a slice of blackened toast. He scowled at Greta, who stood round-shouldered and oblivious before the bulwark of his desk, her lips parted slightly.

"I completed my part of the bargain. Do you have any idea how difficult negotiating with an Englishman is right now? It's a diplomatic nightmare. And Willoughby-Jones—the fool—wanted to charge more, because two of the things died in transit. That's not my problem!" Lothar's angular face was white and pinched, his thin moustache pointed sharply downward. Features frozen, the telephone pressed to his head, he listened to Herr Gunn. Greta's shallow breaths were the only sound. The Fuhrenmanns held this tense tableau until at last Lothar broke the stillness with a sudden harsh bark.

"I'll give you two days to secure a minimum of half a dozen bookings for the bear. No more excuses. The war will proceed. Life will proceed. I will continue to owe my creditors. The panda eats its weight in bamboo and fruit every three days – do you have any idea how expensive that is? Call me when you have the bookings." Lothar used two hands to replace the phone and end the call, then he turned his white, beak-like nose toward his wife.

"What is it, Frau Fuhrenmann? You disturb me greatly."

"It is Happy, Herr Fuhrenmann. He has vomited up his breakfast."

"So clean it up."

"Yes, I have cleaned it. However, the bear is acting unwell."

"Acting unwell," echoed Lothar. "How unspecific. Please explain."

"He is groaning, and shaking his head, and he isn't moving much," Greta reported. She stood before her husband's desk, lumpish and resigned. Her dress, Lothar recalled, had been white and dotted with pale pink flowers at some time in the past. It was now a mottled ochre. What had he done to anger God? His wife was a dowdy numbskull, his children were incorrigible, and his career was a joke. Each day he rose, washed, trimmed, combed, dressed, waxed, and polished. He was a devout man, who said his prayers to ask forgiveness for whatever unfathomable sins he had committed. *Great sins they must have been*, thought Lothar, *to bring upon me these burdens.*

Lothar rose violently from his chair, his angular face suddenly separated from Greta's wide, pale cheeks by only inches. She raised her eyebrows slightly and flinched. He made a noise, a guttural, inchoate threat that died at his lips, then pushed past his wife.

Lothar marched out of his house. He followed a gravel path to a padlocked gate on a two-meter-high chain-link fence. Barbed wire curled and bristled at the top of the fence. It was a back entrance to the Kolner Zoo, and its proximity had appealed to Lothar Fuhrenmann when he had bought the house, but now he wished he lived as far away as possible from the damn zoo. He wouldn't be tempted to take on so many of the menial tasks and duties associated with the great dumb beasts. How cruel fate had been to lead him into this sorry excuse of a livelihood, displaying a menagerie to a soft-hearted, mush-brained populace. It was a mediocre profit margin at best. Lothar couldn't imagine why he should allow his income to dwindle by employing an incompetent fool to shove food through the bars each day. Did he not have Greta and the children at his disposal?

Gravel crunched under his boots as Lothar strode toward Happy's enclosure. The animal lay on its side, its white fur streaked with brown mud. Was it dead? After surviving a rough capture and transport, had the black-and-white beast chosen to die now, on his watch? No, the thing's sides were heaving. Lothar circled the bars until he found Happy's unfocused, bloodshot eyes.

"You ungrateful shit."

The vomiting was likely due to the excessive fruit-to-bamboo ratio on which Lothar himself had insisted. Of course, he would admit this to no one. The other large animals tolerated inexpensive foodstuffs replacing their native diets, but oh, no. Not this problematic cartoon of a creature.

The zoo wouldn't open for another hour. Lothar scanned over his shoulders. Satisfied no human could see or hear him, he began to kick viciously at the bars of Happy's cage, interspersing his kicks with nasty utterances, spit spraying from his lips and wetting his thin moustache.

Happy the Panda didn't react. The bear was smart. People beyond the steel bars were powerless to harm him.

Yukuai

They use crunchy green bamboo to lure me from one black-barred box to the next. I learned that a move is imminent when they don't feed me, and I become weak with hunger. Men stand outside my box and make harsh, rattling sounds.

They move me in the darkness of night, in a rolling machine baited with sweet bamboo. In my desperate, famished state, I go wherever they want me to go: into the rolling man machine, or anywhere else they place familiar food from my homeland.

Before dawn, the metal doors of my moving prison open and disgorge me into a new black-barred box, free of my own droppings and urine. The sun rises and I explore every corner of the foreign enclosure, searching for a weakness or a flaw—any kind of way out. Then the humans arrive—whole crowds pushing, pointing, shouting, crying, spitting, and calling out.

In my dreams, I return to clear streams of laughing water, fine mists of rain delicately irrigating green grasses and trees, and moisture from the sky revealing the nature of rocks and earth. Time passes, and these dreams grow faint and infrequent.

I have been in this, what seems to be my final penitentiary, for a long time now, without any movement or change. Somehow I have left the spitting men behind, the men and she-men here speak soft and low. For this small mercy, at least, I can be grateful.

Kitimat

Gilbert hovered in the wings of an outdoor stage all morning. He found a mossy old cedar stump to sit on, and watched Moksgm'ol splash in the river and slap fish to shore, unzip their slippery skins with a skillful claw, lick up their pink flesh. He returned home some time after noon, walking slowly, peacefully, through the forest. In spite of his poor sleep he felt renewed, invigorated, and after a brief lunch of cold water, bread, and fruit in his cabin, he went outside to split wood in the intense fall sunshine.

Gilbert loved the efficient ballet of the woodpile, the upward heft of the axe or maul, smooth wooden handle sliding freely between his calloused palms as it described a graceful parabola. He loved the decisive moment of gravity and intention at the apex of the swing, and the loud, gratifying whack of metal wedge into round wooden rings. He loved the predictable physics of hewn wood pieces flying off in opposite directions, and the intermittent pauses when he stacked quantities of perfectly split wood into rows and pyramids of fuel.

Throwing his shirt carelessly aside, Gilbert settled into rhythmic labour. Moments of idyllic perfection can pass unconsidered, but Gilbert noted the gift of this day, and captured it like an insect in amber. He swung his axe in the autumn of his own existence on the Great Mother. He had grown children, Max and Charlotte. They lived nearby, Charlotte with her husband and child, and Max on his own. Charlotte was pregnant with his second grandchild. Jack, the first, was three years old, boisterous, demanding, and perennially dirty. Max lived alone. He was quiet, verging on sullen, and worked at a tire shop in Kitimat. Their mother, Gilbert's wife Clara, had succumbed to cancer six years earlier. These days, when Gilbert thought of Clara, he felt blessed. He recalled the good times. He didn't dwell on the illness, and how it had leached joy from their lives.

The oil pipeline project was announced two years after Clara died. Gilbert redirected his anger and grief. He turned them toward the government, the oil company, and those who approved of the pipeline, including his son Max. Being busy helped Gilbert bury Clara. There were meetings to plan for and attend, protests to organize, and facts, statistics, and research to consider and compile. Ultimately, it had all been for naught. Then there was the gross affront and indignity of the actual construction of the pipeline. Some days, if the wind was coming from the northeast, Gilbert heard the grind and crunch of machinery and the crash of falling timber. He smelled diesel and dirt all day. The events were close enough in time that he couldn't help but compare them: Clara's death had been easier to handle than the coming of the Black Snake.

None of these difficult thoughts crowded Gilbert's head that glorious autumn afternoon. Tawny skin shone with sweat, taut muscles stretched and worked. Gary and Sandra pulled up in front of the cabin in their small white pickup truck, its faulty exhaust announcing their visit. Gilbert continued swinging and whacking, though he knew his friends were there.

"Maybe put your shirt on, before my wife leaves me," Gary called out the open passenger window.

Gilbert let the axe fall by his side. He looked up. "Water," he said, and went into the cabin. When he came back he was wearing a t-shirt and carrying three tall glasses of ice water. Gary and Sandra sat on the tailgate of their truck, smoking. Gilbert distributed the water wordlessly. All three of them sat for some minutes without speaking, listening to the buzz of a chainsaw half a kilometre away, and the sawing of crickets in the roadside grass.

"Cold winter coming," said Gary.

"Maybe." Gilbert cocked his head to one side and smiled at his friend.

"Must be a cold winter coming." Gary pointed at the stack of split wood.

"Maybe," Gilbert said. "Maybe it's just a good day to split wood. What do you see from the sky these days?"

Gary was a bush pilot. He often brought news about land being cleared, houses being built, or herds of deer passing through.

Gary shrugged. "Not much these days. More tankers anchored off-shore than I've ever seen. Makes me damn nervous."

The thought of oil supertankers navigating the winding archipelago in his backyard made Gilbert nervous, too.

"I'm done worrying," he lied.

"When is Charlotte's baby due?" asked Sandra.

"Soon. Harvest moon."

"Any names?" Sandra arched an eyebrow.

"River, for a boy. Ocean, for a girl." Gilbert grinned. "I suggested Eddy and Swell, for middle names. Charlotte didn't think it was funny."

"It's funny," Sandra laughed.

"If you want to fly with me before the snow comes, then you should come soon," Gary offered.

"Thanks," said Gilbert. "Maybe I will."

Gary and Sandra ground out their cigarettes in the grass and said goodbye. A cough of blue exhaust puffed into the street when Sandra started the truck. Disgusted, Gilbert made a face and shooed them away with the back of his hand.

In the rear-view mirror, Sandra watched Gilbert pick up his axe and return to his woodpile.

"He's lonely," she said. Gary nodded.

Birds and Bees

The blade of a bulldozer dislodged a rock, and that rock nudged a bigger rock, and that rock pounded into the pipeline without puncturing it. The pipeline was compromised, a dent pushed into a thick green plastic cylinder. For a time, nothing happened. The construction crew above the pipeline kept working on the hotel and housing complex they were building. Nothing was visibly amiss. But underground, pressure was building. Gritty, unrefined bitumen worked at the pipe's injury, wearing away at the weakened place.

Oil under pressure found the path of least resistance and then—*Pow! Ka-Blam!*—there was a geyser. Black liquid bored a hole through loosely packed earth above it. It gushed into open air and splattered on the ground; it splashed and pooled and flowed.

This happened in a small forested area between the Kitimat town centre and the Kitimat River. When a pipeline ruptures in the forest, does anybody hear? It happened at night. Nearby businesses had closed for the day. The builders on the construction site had long since hung up their hard hats and headed home.

Worms choked, roots withered, and a puddle became a pool, a pond, a lake. Morning came, and the smell in the air felled the bees. It fouled the bees. It confused, sickened, and grounded the bees. Birds flew away, fearful of the invisible, toxic vapours.

KITIMAT

The smell reached him in his dreams.

He was dreaming about the days when the kids were small. In the dream, it was summertime. He was pushing Max on a tire swing. Charlotte was suspended from a knotted rope, on the far side of the same splendid, spreading tree that held the swing. Max kicked his dirty bare feet toward the clouds, his mouth open. *Higher, daddy, higher,* he demanded. Charlotte's curtain of black-brown hair whooshed around her serene face. She was wearing a soft green dress that she had worn every day, it seemed, for a year or two. He could hear the sounds of other children laughing and screeching. A dog barked incessantly. An internal combustion engine operating far away made a faint mechanical roar.

Max grew more insistent in the dream, screaming his frustrated demand.

Higher, Daddy. Higher, higher!

Gilbert pushed the tire absentmindedly. Where was that roaring engine sound coming from? There must be a vehicle somewhere, but he couldn't see it. An odour of raw, dirty fuel grew pungent in the playground. The mechanical sound came from everywhere, and nowhere. *Higher, daddy. Higher!* screamed Max, hysterical. Gilbert turned to his son.

Oily tears were streaming down Max's face, coursing from empty black eyes. Two inky lines stained the collar of the boy's yellow T-shirt. Gilbert looked at Charlotte. She had stopped swinging. She hung motionless, black rivulets of oil flowing down her face, ruining the favourite green dress.

An overpowering smell of fuel choked him, and Gilbert woke up, gasping. He threw the covers off of his body, rejecting the dream, but the reek of oil permeated his house. Outside cars whooshed by, and a siren wailed in the distance.

No. Gilbert grabbed his jeans, ripped a shirt from his closet, and pushed his feet into runners. He stumbled outside, his hair wild from tossing and turning, his eyes wide. *No.*

Gary was sitting in his truck in front of Gilbert's house, idling the engine. Gilbert felt angry relief – here was the cause of the powerful stench, Gary's piece-of-shit truck. But across the street, Gilbert's neighbours were standing in their front yards, talking, looking toward town, and glancing back at his cabin. Everyone knew how hard Gilbert had fought against the pipeline. The single siren became an orchestra of emergency vehicle alarms, a spiralling cacophony.

Gary's face was a flat, impassive mask. He stared blankly out the windshield. Gilbert's stomach clenched, his lungs felt tight and unresponsive. It had happened, already. This soon after the construction of the pipeline, the disaster that they had tried to avert was here, happening now. Gilbert climbed into Gary's truck.

The drive took less than five minutes. They headed west of downtown on Haisla Boulevard, toward the bridge that spanned the Kitimat River. A semicircle of haphazardly parked emergency vehicles, fire trucks and police cars, blocked the road. Dozens of people in blue coveralls and day-glo orange-and-yellow crossed work vests wandered near a housing development that was under construction beside a little strip mall. The development, spindly wooden frames, some partially covered in particleboard, was spread out over an expanse of brown mud.

Knots of people had collected beside the emergency vehicles, some frowning and some weeping, most holding shirts or scraps of fabric over their mouths and noses. The smell was overpowering. Gilbert got out of the truck, his eyes watering, fumes thick in the air, despair thick in his heart. Scraps of comments peppered with obscenities reached him underneath the sirens. White pickup trucks circled the perimeter of the scene, a swirly green logo identifying them as oil company vehicles.

The pipeline was long. Kitimat was the Black Snake's tail. It stretched over a thousand kilometres to the fangs and forked tongue of its hungry mouth in Alberta. A spill could have happened anywhere along that length, but it had happened here, in Gilbert's backyard. He imagined a crystal vase falling onto a tile floor and smashing spectacularly, a hundred thousand splinters of clear glass skittering into corners, a tiny rainbow in each shard, sharp specks of crystal buried in cracks, undetected until a hapless bare foot or a child's curious hand discovered them, sharp shock of pain, blood welling up.

"Half a kilometre from the river," said Gary.

"If that," said Gilbert.

The spilled oil was invisible from Haisla Boulevard, only the chemical, lung-searing smell gave it away. Images from media coverage of other spills crowded Gilbert's mind, black puddles clogging wetlands and coating plant life, birds with their feathers glued together, robbed of flight and dignity, enduring hose baths, detergents, attempts to reverse the torture. Fish would follow, washed up on gooey black banks, their gills fused, eyes popping, asphyxiated. And so it would go, filtering up the food chain, until it built up in the carnivores, the eagles and the bears.

Peter Langston—a member of Kitimat's tiny television news team—elbowed his way through the crowd when he saw Gilbert, brandishing a microphone, and flanked by a cameraman.

"You predicted it, Gilbert. Want to go on the record, and say 'I told you so'?" Peter smiled brightly.

Gilbert glared past the journalist. He was silent; he had turned to stone.

"Can't blame a guy for trying," Peter sighed. "On me," he directed. The cameraman obediently swung around and focused his lens on the journalist.

"In the early hours of this morning, a woman walking her dog noticed a strong smell of oil. She alerted the Kitimat Fire Department, who came to investigate. They found a large pool of oil accumulating behind this downtown housing development. Officials at Elba Energy have confirmed that the pipeline they installed last year has ruptured, just north of here. There is no estimate available yet as to the size of the spill. However, Elba Energy spokesperson Lily Perch says that cleanup crews have been mobilized, and they are focusing on keeping the spill from reaching the Kitimat River, which flows just one hundred meters away. The cause of the pipeline rupture is not yet known."

Gilbert heard the mournful chanting of his people and the loud, low, sombre beat of a funeral drum. It could have been live music, or maybe he was conjuring up his own internal soundtrack to the spill. He walked along the taped-off perimeter of the tragedy, breathing through a folded t-shirt, seeking a glimpse of wet, black oil the way motorists peer into highway carnage for a thrill of bright red blood.

His spirit walked beside him, outside his skin. He noted his calm with numb curiosity. He supposed all his fire had burned up in the fight to stop the pipeline from being built. A spill was inevitable, so he had acted as if it had already happened, way back when he and his fellow anti-pipeline activists were blocking roads, hefting placards, and chaining themselves to bulldozers. He wasn't inspired to leap into action and help the cleanup crews. He knew that oil spills, like big car accidents, leave irreparable damage and destruction in their wake. A child without a seatbelt who is paralyzed after a head-on collision needs help learning to navigate life in a wheelchair, and psychological counselling to become philosophical, but nothing will return the use of his or her legs. This pristine waterway, these precious plants and animals, the grand and glorious ecosystem Gilbert and his ancestors called home—all of this was irrevocably tainted, damaged into a future day that might never come.

White cumulus clouds sailed inland against a field of brilliant blue. A yellow and black school bus rumbled by, making its quotidian rounds. A helicopter chattered overhead, hovering above the forest. One by one the sirens wound down, their pitches petering out, giving up. Gilbert stood beside a line of yellow police tape, blinking. The emptiness, a hopeless black hole, opened up in him as it had when Clara died. One of the orange-vested workers shouted in the forest. Gilbert squinted in the direction of the shout, and for a second he thought he saw the flash of Moksgm'ol's blonde back, fleeing across the highway.

MOKSGM'OL

I wake, and a vile man-smell assails my nostrils. It is a sharp, sour smell, similar to the stench of their rock-hard paths, but worse. Behind the big smell there are other scents, not forest, not river, not fish, not bear, not earth, and not tree. It is an assault of man-smells. I remain motionless, except for my ears, which I cock up, and turn in the direction of the stink.

Men blunder in the trees to the west, blocking one escape. There are other ways to escape from here, all dangerous, and strewn with strange man-things. But I cannot wait until the men retreat, and they crash ever closer to the fall-berry place I, Moksgm'ol, have always known.

The stench is intolerable. I begin to pick my escape, moving cautiously between fern and forest. Gusts of wind from the wide salt water push sounds and smells toward me—then the wind changes, and I must stop again, to choose a new way. The wind whips around and, impossibly, there is a man in front of me. I rear up on my hind legs, and roar my displeasure. Be gone man! I am Moksgm'ol! Be gone! She does not move. It is a female man – I smell her blood – I am Moksgm'ol, be gone!

Running I am running crushing crashing wanting away from the man, and then there are more men. The stink again, it assaults my senses, I veer to find another way! I come upon a line of yellow metal machines and a rock-hard path, and I turn and crash across it, my claws clicking on the strange surface. Men cry out, they have seen Moksgm'ol, I feel their senses turn toward me and I must run! I must use speed to break beyond the man-barriers. I cannot see. I am crashing around, crashing through. I want only the quiet green of a man-less forest. I only want to be away from men. I only want to be somewhere that is for bears.

Churchill

News of the oil spill in Kitimat didn't reach the staff of the Churchill Northern Studies Centre until the day after the pipeline ruptured.

They woke early that day to collect field data as a team, ate a hearty breakfast, collected cameras, equipment, safety gear, and cold weather clothing, then struck out on foot into Wapusk National Park. Jane noted the exceptionally good visibility afforded by the weather conditions, cold and cloudless. They sighted twelve bears in rapid succession, including one particularly malnourished sow who hadn't been seen for ten weeks. The team had feared the worst. Anne was first to spot her.

"There's Tlingit!" Anne whisper-yelled, pressing binoculars to her face with one hand, and pointing with the other.

"Well, I'll be darned," said Ian, following the line of Anne's extended arm and spotting the skinny bear.

"It's too distant for positive identification," said Jane.

Anne lowered the binoculars and turned to Jane, who hadn't even looked up from her notebook. She was jotting in point-form, meticulously recording temperature, snow pack conditions, and confirmed bear sightings. Contempt for her colleague overwhelmed Anne with a sudden ferocity, and she whipped the binoculars in front of Jane's eyes, pushed them into her eye sockets, and forced the woman's face upward.

"Look for yourself." Anne was flushed, scarlet.

"Ow – stop – that *hurts!*"

"Hey, hey, now, take it easy, ladies. Anne, get a grip. Jane, have a look. I'm pretty sure Anne is right, Jane. That's Tlingit."

Ian checked the bear's markings and confirmed the sighting, but the damage was done. Jane returned to her notebook in haughty, martyred silence. Anne trudged along, heavy with remorse. Both women ignored Ian's valiant attempts at cheerfulness.

"What a stunning day. Clearest this month, wouldn't you say? And it's warming up!"

The bog underfoot had a crusty, thin top layer of ice. Their footsteps crunched with each step, and small mammals scattered at their approach. The bog was a high, partly-frozen table of water and vegetation. It provided ideal denning sites for polar bears. Ian nattered about topographical changes caused by the warming climate, and Anne half-listened to his dismal predictions. If the permafrost below the bog thawed, the bog would become a fen, a swampy area unsuitable for bears, too wet to get around in without fins and gills, or wings.

Hours ticked by. The sun moved overhead, and their footsteps began to squish instead of crunch. Ian held up his hand, signalling a halt. The stretched smile of forced optimism he had worn all morning disappeared.

Jane busied herself with her notebook. Anne flirted with apologizing, but the words got stuck in her throat, because she wasn't actually sorry. Ian shuffled his nylon zip bag off his shoulder and extracted an aluminum tripod, a survey camera, and a collapsible depth-measurement stick. His long, skinny limbs matched his tools, extendable apparatuses reaching from land to sky. He got tangled up in the tripod legs, dropped his bag, and windmilled his arms to catch his balance. He looked like a silent-film slapstick star, and despite her low mood Anne pressed her lips together to stifle a giggle.

Ian untangled himself, and Anne wandered away from her colleagues, scanning the horizon methodically—as she did every day here in Manitoba—for her beloved bears. Occasionally, she glanced back at Ian, his face hidden in his giant parka hood, and Jane, scribbling her notes, as if she weren't standing in an icefield surrounded by polar bears. They measured and counted, tabulated and calculated, but there was no mystery. They were all here in Churchill on forgone conclusions. The planet was warming up, the polar bear's habitat was shrinking. The precise amount of prime bog real estate reduced to soggy fen hardly seemed to matter. Less habitat for Ian to survey, fewer starving, homeless bears for Anne to count – but plenty of data for Jane to plug into her computer, to generate bar graphs, pie charts, and exponential curves.

The sun scoured the landscape, merciless in the solid blue sky. Ice melted, insidious trickling of countless little drops. The little expedition that had been so merry in the morning was a grim trio by late afternoon. Hair clung to their foreheads, slick with sweat, and they were splattered with warm, wet mud from ankles to knees. Anne sighed as they approached the square, geometric sprawl of the research centre buildings.

"My grandmother would have called this a damn fine day," Ian said, "but these bears would disagree. Should we debrief at dinner?"

Anne grunted an assent.

"I'm not coming to dinner. I'll present my findings over breakfast tomorrow," said Jane.

Anne wrestled internally, a tug-of-war between crushing guilt for assaulting her colleague, a woman both smaller and older than herself, and pleasure that she wouldn't have to deal with Jane's stilted, wooden company until the following day.

Less than half an hour later, Anne was spreading a slab of white bread with a generous dollop of blueberry jam when she heard Ian yelling from the common room. She balanced the toast and jam in one hand and jogged awkwardly down the hall to the common room, and then the three scientists were suddenly together again, standing incredulous before the centre's lone television.

Anne knew about the Elba Energy Company's oil pipeline from Alberta to British Columbia's Pacific coast, and she abhorred it. Spirit bears, the other white bears, were in peril because of that pipeline. One spill, and the bears' forests, rivers and coastline would be fouled, their diet poisoned, their habitat devastated. But modern pipeline technology was safe, Elba Energy maintained. Industry standards were rigorous. All interested parties had carried out extensive research and development. Precautions were in place.

And yet. Sickeningly familiar images flashed on the television screen, the hallmarks of environmental disaster: face masks, yellow tape, workers in haz-mat suits, clusters of horrified onlookers, and the oil itself, extending a black finger into the Kitimat River, fracturing light into dark rainbows.

Tears sprang to Anne's eyes as the impact of the spill sank in. She glanced at her colleagues. Ian's mouth was opening and closing, rhythmically and convulsively, like a fish gasping for breath. Jane was unreadable. Her mouth was a straight line and her brown eyes were flat and lightless.

It was breaking news, few details were available. The local reporter's zeal gave away poorly suppressed excitement. He had bushy eyebrows that bounced up and down, punctuating his report. The pipeline had ruptured near a construction site. Oil was flowing into a forested area in the centre of Kitimat, the harbour city where massive supertankers docked, filled up with oil, then navigated a narrow waterway to the Pacific ocean. The reporter turned his attention to one of the onlookers, a man he identified as *Mister Gilbert Crow*, and demanded to know the man's opinion.

The proud, serious face of a middle-aged native man filled the screen. He was handsome, thought Anne. Gorgeous, really – black hair hung loose around a tanned, linear face, the features strong and balanced.

Whoever Mister Crow was, he didn't speak. He stared beyond the camera, beyond Kitimat, and beyond the clouds. His black eyes seemed to stare across the country, from a shore on the Pacific northwest coast all the way to the shore of Hudson Bay in Manitoba. His stare found Anne, and in his fathomless eyes she recognized a tactic that she herself employed, a hardening in the face of adversity. Beside her, Jane sniffed, a delicate, tiny sound that nevertheless pulled Anne's attention from the screen.

Jane's eyes were lost, too, just like Mister Crow's; they were everywhere and nowhere. Maybe Jane wasn't as cold, callous and indifferent as Anne had some time ago concluded. Perhaps Anne had been unfair in her estimation of Jane. *Great, something else to plague my conscience.* Anne took an enormous, mournful bite of her toast, and a blob of blueberry jam glopped onto her shirt.

HIGHWAY 16

Jonathan began packing to head north and help clean up the spill the same day he heard about it. He shared a house on East 12th Street in Vancouver with four other guys, and his rent was paid up for September. He was close to his monthly quota soliciting advertisers for *The Georgia Straight*, a popular urban entertainment weekly. It wasn't, in any case, the pinnacle of his career ambitions. He had no girlfriend and no pets, not even a house plant – he was free to pick up and go, though his bank account was a little slim. It was raining in Vancouver, and he was overdue for a road trip.

Jonathan reduced, reused, and recycled. He rode his bicycle, and used public transportation. The Volvo wagon he wanted to borrow was his mother's second car; hopefully she didn't need it for a few days, so he could make the eight-hundred-kilometre drive to Kitimat. He was an environmentalist, and he tried to look the part: long, lanky hair, casual outdoor sports clothes, whale tattoo on his right forearm. He was picking away at college courses, circling a geography degree, with a minor in environmental sustainability. He thought about his great-grandfather a lot, and it gave him an extra edge. Jonathan didn't only want to save the planet; he also wanted to atone for the sins of his Nazi-sympathizing, panda-abusing, right-wing bastard of an ancestor.

When Jonathan was a little boy he saw pictures of his great-grandfather, Lothar, in the same frame as a large, live panda bear. His childish impression was one of benevolence: *Great-grandpa liked animals! He ran a zoo!* Jonathan's family had lived and worked in and around Cologne, Germany, for centuries. In their basement den, his parents displayed memorabilia from the Kolner Zoo in Cologne. There was a framed map of the zoo, and prints of posters advertising various special exhibits: African Safari at the Kolner Zoo, Underwater Adventure at the Kolner Zoo, Happy the Giant Panda at the Kolner Zoo. This last poster included Lothar and his tight smile. Gradually, by way of photo-album explanations and dinner-table anecdotes, the story of happy-granddaddy-zookeeper eroded, and the bones of the man showed through.

At eleven years old, Jonathan learned about the Holocaust from his parents. They weren't deniers. They held a liberal, no-excuses perspective, but since their son was young and impressionable, they minimized it. Not the reality of the war or its horrors, but their family's participation.

Jonathan invented a story about how his great-grandfather had survived living in Nazi Germany. Lothar Fuhrenmann had immersed himself in the animal kingdom, thereby pushing away the grim politics of his nation. He had spent guiltless days promoting animal exhibits, acquiring and caring for exotic creatures, tenderly feeding them rations obtained with difficulty – bravery, even. His wife, Greta, had kept the home fires burning, put the schnitzel on the table, read the kids to sleep with animal stories, laundered the white shirts—white, not brown—and pressed and hung them with characteristic German precision in Lothar's armoire.

Fifteen-year-old Jonathan was lurking at the perimeter of one of his parents' prolonged, wine-infused dinner parties when he first heard about the human exhibits. His father had made a disparaging comment about Asian drivers in Vancouver, a not-uncommon stereotype.

"Careful, Bernie," his mother slurred. "Remember your heritage."

"I'm not a racist; it's observable fact," his father answered.

"Bernie's grandfather put people in zoos," his mother offered up to the general conversation.

"What do you mean, put them in zoos?" a guest asked.

"He ran a zoo, and they had *human exhibits.* Bernie's grandfather got ahold of some native people, dressed them up in feathers and rawhide, and charged admission!"

"It was a common occurrence at the time, Hilary," said his father.

"So was genocide."

Jonathan retreated as the argument escalated.

The next morning, his mother—her face a mask of chalk, hands shaking beside her coffee—regarded him with the mute resentment of the seriously hung over. He scrambled eggs, drank a carton of milk, and whistled the melody of his current favourite song, blithely ignoring all the warning signs of one of his mother's poisonous moods.

"Did Great-granddad really put people in zoos?"

"Oh, for Christ's sake."

"Well, did he?"

She sighed, hung her head, and looked up at him from puffy, bloodshot eyes.

"Yes, he did. He was a Nazi sympathizer. He was an opportunist. He gauged public sentiment, and gambled that white people would pay to see brown people behind bars."

"Wow. That sucks."

Jonathan asked a lot of questions over the next week, and the answers he got were pretty depressing. He began to investigate, tentatively, on the internet, and soon he found himself reading about the Allied Forces' firebombing of Cologne, on the thirtieth and the thirty-first of May, 1942. The bombing had—miraculously—never been discussed in Jonathan's presence, even though he wouldn't be alive, if Lothar, Greta and their children hadn't survived the raid.

It was a thousand-bomber raid, codenamed Operation Millennium. A thousand bombers! The sky must have black with them, like a plague of giant deadly insects. The raid was supposed to be devastating enough to damage German morale, maybe even smack Germany right out of the war. But the firebombing resulted in just short of five hundred deaths. About five thousand people were injured, and over twelve thousand buildings damaged or destroyed.

Jonathan's father was visibly uncomfortable with his son's research. He ignored the facts his son presented to him at regular intervals. Often, he wouldn't even deign to lower the newspaper blocking his face to deliver his curt replies.

"What happened to the animals?" Jonathan asked one day.

Bernard slowly lowered his newspaper and regarded his son expressionlessly.

"What animals?"

"The animals in the Kolner zoo. What happened to them?"

Bernard momentarily furrowed his brow and then answered flatly, "They died, I expect."

"Why didn't anyone try to save them?"

"The city was on fire, Jonathan. There were human lives to save. I don't suppose anything could have been done about the animals." The newspaper ascended, end of discussion.

Jonathan could picture it, an apocalypse of fire raining down, without precedent or explanation. The animals must have been terrified, their situation somehow more gruesome and horrible than the humans' because of their captivity. There was nowhere to run, and nowhere to hide. The citizens of Cologne had the context of the war, the knowledge that their nation was besieged. Attacks were likely, to be expected. There must have been sirens wailing at the sound of the approaching enemy airplanes. The people of Cologne could have tried to run for shelter in basements, or flee the city, on foot or in vehicles. But the animals locked in cages at the zoo...

What had Lothar Fuhrenmann done that night? Perhaps he had run heroically from cage to cage, a great ring of skeleton keys in his hand, yanking open barred enclosures and calling to the animals, encouraging them to run for their lives. What had *actually* happened? Jonathan squirmed. His intuition told him the truth was something wrong, something shameful.

Dawn broke on the thirty-first of May, 1942, though the smoke was too thick for sunlight to reach what was left of Cologne. The horizon glowed orange and red from fires that were still burning. Lothar Fuhrenmann was the only human soul on the Kolner Zoo premises, there were no witnesses. Some of the enclosures had been spared, others were just black smears on the ground. The peacock garden, for example, with its delicate wooden fence, was only a memory. A smell of roast chicken lingered there. Distant crashes, sirens, and screams came from far away. Lothar strode directly to Happy's cage. The bear was pacing, whimpering pathetically, its beady eyes rolling. Lothar fingered the irregular edges of two objects in his front trouser pocket: a metal key, and a loaded handgun. When the bear saw him it became much more agitated, swaying frantically at the door of its enclosure, red-rimmed eyes exploding from their sockets. Lothar slowed to a saunter, stopping close to the bear's dirty muzzle. He leaned toward the animal, clenching fists and teeth.

"Fuck you, you fucking Chinese pig-bear. Useless waste of time and money. Thanks for nothing. I hope enjoyed your incineration as much as your incarceration." Lothar turned his back on Happy and walked away, boot heels clicking.

After his research, a new version of his heritage descended on Jonathan. It enveloped him, scratchy and uncomfortable, a hair shirt. Goodbye bratwurst and black forest cake, Hansel and Gretel. Hello brown shirts, barricades, cattle cars, crying children, and firing squads.

Cologne, Germany

Cringing in the crawl space under the house, Lothar and his family survived the firebombing of Cologne, although their home did not. They heard explosions, and anguished screams for help. His children blubbered nonstop, and begged to leave the safety of the basement. Dire rumbles, the crashing of collapsing buildings, and the wailing of countless sirens made Lothar insist his family remain huddled in the dirty half-cellar. At last, Herr Fuhrenmann could take the snivelling no longer, and imposed silence. Greta drew her children to her ample bosom, one tousled blonde head under each arm. Dust and tiny rocks disgorged from above them, dirtying their hair and clothes, sticking to tracks of tears on the children's cheeks.

But they survived, as Lothar had gambled they would, huddled under the house. He grinned at his family, fiercely triumphant.

I will begin again, after tonight, he thought. No more zoos, animals, shit, straw, feathers, or fur. No more courting the public, that horrible bitch, no more trying to separate the ignorant masses from their money. He would walk out of this country a refugee, and start again. He would go to Canada, and hack an existence out of the wilderness. He would farm, the way his ancestors had. Farming was an honest, noble profession. He would raise animals, and he would slaughter them for their meat. Greta and his children could follow him, if they wished to. He wouldn't shirk his duties as a man and a father.

Morning arrived in eerie silence. The children and Greta slept, propped up in a corner under a layer of filth. It took some doing, because of the rubble piled on top of it, but Lothar kicked and kicked until the heavy slatted basement door opened, revealing a grey expanse of ash, smoke, and dust. The streets were unrecognizable, littered with bodies, chunks of buildings, and burnt debris. Lothar picked his way through what was left of Cologne, surveying the death and destruction with satisfaction. His life here was finished, all he needed was seed money to get started overseas.

He took a necessarily circuitous route, and picked his way into the zoo to inspect his investments. *If any of those dumb, godforsaken beasts are still alive, I'll sell them.* He wasn't afraid of the big feline predators—lions, tigers, or panthers. They wouldn't be running wild, free of their bombed cages, because Lothar himself had put bullets in their skulls the night before. Any docile beasts worth enough money he had spared, the giraffes and the elephant, the snakes, ostriches and emus. He hadn't shown Happy the same mercy as the big cats, partly because he didn't believe the bear was dangerous, but mostly because the panda had caused him so much trouble. That Chinese bear had given back so little, for all the trouble it had caused every step of the way: finding a dealer, purchasing the bear, paying for its transport, feeding and housing it. He resented the black and white beast, and he wanted it to suffer.

The Kolner Zoo was a mess. There were blackened craters where cages used to be. Twisted metal bars curved and pointed in odd directions. He heard unidentified animals squeaking for help, but didn't follow up on the sounds. He made his way to Happy's enclosure.

At first, he was certain Happy was dead. The cage wasn't compromised, and the bear was there, a mound of matted fur lying in a great lump. A heart attack maybe, or shrapnel from a nearby explosion. But then the animal moved, rolled up to sitting and stared at Lothar, bleary-eyed and stunned. Happy snuffled, his piggish eyes focused, and the bear began to pace frantically behind the sooty bars of his cage. Lothar had never seen the panda so animated. It was as if the bear were begging to be released.

"Gott verdammt," breathed Lothar. "You're alive. You big, stupid, lucky animal."

He spent another minute telling the panda precisely what he thought of it, then executed an about-face and went in search of a working telephone, patting the left breast pocket of his zoo uniform jacket. Yes, there it was: the paper with the American name and telephone number scrawled on it. *Anthony Ferguson, Saint Louis Zoo.* Ferguson, the purchaser for the Missouri Zoo, was a damn cheapskate—at least, Lothar had thought so, until today. Yesterday, an animal purchase would have had to pass through the correct channels, and paperwork would have had to be completed, according to rigorous specifications. Who was there to watch over a purchase today? *Fire sale!* The money – all of it – could be deposited directly into Lothar's personal account, and no one would be the wiser. All he needed was a telephone.

A long, strangled cry pierced the air. Lothar gazed absently around what was left of the Kolner Zoo. Then he stepped over the rubble of his past, bursting with satisfaction, closing this miserable chapter in his life.

"Make me some money, Happy."

YUKUAI

The combined scat of a multitude of animals—I smell it every morning. Before opening my eyes, I know everything is the same. I am still a prisoner, I am still not free. Was I ever free, or was it all a dream, those wet green fields of my homeland, those other bears like me?

My chalky pool of fetid water is dotted with brown leaves today, which is a different thing. I will investigate. I roll onto my paws and stretch. I smell the grass I slept on. Naturally, I want to hide my scent, but there is nothing to scratch over the spot, and nowhere to hide. Many of my urges are thwarted, futile or impossible. Still the urges persist, so the dream must have been real. Why do I want to hide the place I sleep, hide where I scat? I long to flee from the men and their young, who stand too close and shout at me. At some time, it must have been possible to run away.

The rolling thing with the man-who-brings-bamboo arrives. It is noisy, and it smells foul, but it brings bamboo. He stops the rolling thing and takes the bamboo from it, but instead of throwing me my bamboo, he stands and speaks. He stares at me in my prison, like all of the other men do.

I like different things if they are pleasant, but this is not. I want the man to shut up and throw the bamboo. Finally, he does. I fall upon it, crunchy juice and wet stalks at last!

The speaking is not good. It reminds me of another man, another prison, another night, long ago. It was the Firenight. The cruel man spat hate at me through the bars. I do not understand the speech of men, but I feel goodness, and I feel cruelty. I know the difference between the child who speaks in gentle tones of wonder, and the child who makes sure that no one is watching when he throws a rock.

The foul, spitting man was full of hatred. He would have killed me if he could.

Kitimat

Walking home, the smell and the noise faded out, receded with every step. Cars slowed beside him. Some people spoke to him and called his name, or offered to drive him home, including Gary in his beat-up white truck. Gilbert acknowledged no one. The blackness had descended on him, as thick and dark as when Clara died. *Walking away I am walking away I am walking, walking, walking.* He kept his eyes straight ahead. He focused on nothing, because he saw nothing.

At his cabin, he left his shoes on the porch and went inside, closing the door gingerly behind him. He went into his bedroom, stretched out in the exact centre of his bed, crossed his arms over his chest, and examined the irregularities in the ceiling. He used to lie in this meditative, supine position when he missed Clara, trying to conjure her presence beside him, in the bed that they used to share. Every tiny fissure of the ceiling was familiar to him—every bump, every crack, and every discolouration. His eyes wandered over the topography of sorrow above him. His mind was still numb.

The days and nights that he had spent heating his mental forge and hammering out solutions were over. There was no more fuel to feed the fire that had roared beneath Gilbert's passionate bid to stop the pipeline. Gilbert had tried to save Clara's life, tried to halt the construction of the pipeline. He had tried, and failed. There would be more spills, more pipelines, more deaths, and he was powerless to stop them all.

In his early twenties, Gilbert worked for a tree planting company. He took the job with a sense of nobility. He remembered feeling like a steward of the land, a caretaker of his ancestors. Then one day while he was planting, a white man told him the story of Sisyphus, a Greek guy who was condemned to roll a rock up a hill eternally, only to have it roll back down, over and over, until the end of time.

"*Sisyphus* would be a great name for a tree planting company," the man laughed. "Doesn't matter how many millions we plant, they're gonna be browsed by deer, dead from an insect infestation, or cut down again. Look! You can see the whole cycle from here."

Gilbert stopped planting and leaned on his shovel. It was true. Machinery buzzed and smashed on a distant hillside, clear-cutting virgin forest, removing every stick. Rough roads zigzagged across a brown, uneven landscape: the earth mother, flayed and skinned. The surrounding hills were a patchwork of forest in various stages of rape and decay. There was a yellow triangle where a plantation was failing, a pale green rectangle of young trees struggling to survive, and more brown patches where the logging was fresh and the earth cried out mutely, *this is wrong*. The fragile seedlings nestled in bags at his waist were destined to become particleboard and toilet paper.

Gilbert wasn't healing the earth, he understood. He was participating in its rape. The gloomy realization reminded him of another story, which he told to the white man.

THE GREAT BEAR PUNISHES PEOPLE

The Great Bear heard the people she had created from brown bear cubs crying out for help, and she went to investigate.

The people had the intelligence and cunning she had given them to survive. Even so, they were immature. They needed skins for clothing, trees for fuel and housing, stones for weapons, and feathers for decoration, and they took all these things wastefully and thoughtlessly. They left animals slaughtered and stripped of their skins, the precious meat of their bodies wasted in decay. There were more bodies than Crow and Raven, the carrion eaters, could possibly use for nourishment. The people felled trees and carved their trunks into canoes, but they left the branches to suffocate the forest floor. They shot down birds with arrows, and the birds toppled from the sky, only to have the largest of their feathers yanked roughly from their bodies. The dead birds were then left to wilt and waste. Even the stone the people chipped for arrowheads was stolen, disrespectfully, from Snake's warming spot, and from the mouths of Fish's rivers.

The people were crying because of the Great Bear's warnings. To warn people of their wastefulness, the Great Bear had sent them droughts and floods. She had diverted herds and flocks so there was no meat to kill for food and skins. She had caused sparks to fly when stones were harvested, and the sparks had started fires that burned down the peoples' villages, forests, and fields. Still, the people did not learn. When the herds and flocks returned, or the forests grew back, the humans once again wasted the earth's precious gifts. The Great Bear saw that people would destroy everything that she had created, unless she taught them a long, hard lesson.

The Great Bear thickened the coats of all of the bears. Then she focused her breath on the frozen place of the White Bears, and she blew the wind, ice, and snow, until the world was covered with a thick layer of ice. Many of the people died, but the Great Bear watched carefully, and ensured that some of them survived. Then slowly, gradually, the Great Bear warmed the world with breath from her body.

After the Ice Age, the people were grateful. This time, they learned to use every part of every animal they sacrificed, every twig and branch of every tree that they chopped down. They even gave thanks for rocks and stones, as they knew these resources could disappear under ice.

In the northern night sky, the constellation called Lynx represents the Great Bear's long, cold breaths blowing across the world. Lynx is overhead during the winter months to remind people that winter might return, and stay a hundred years or more, if they become careless and wasteful with the gifts of the Great Bear.

The lined face of the elder who had told Gilbert this story appeared on his bedroom ceiling, wreathed in smoke. He heard her creaky words, her prophetic conviction rang in his ears. In this time, the Great Bear's people had once again become wasteful – would she punish them again?

Then Gilbert had an epiphany. A hand plunged into his chest and squeezed his heart, his eyes popped, and he exhaled as though his lungs had collapsed. The Great Bear was already meting out her punishment. In terribly symmetry, she was warming the planet instead of cooling it. The ice caps were melting, ocean levels were rising, major cities were flooding, crops were failing, infants and the elderly were dying, and still the mercury climbed, a burning red exponential line. The earth's fate was inevitable. People would extract oil, burn coal, drive cars and fly planes; they would keep their factories chugging until the world was a parched, arid, and hostile place. Only when their lands were uninhabitable would they learn to give thanks for the sun, the wind, the tides and the rain.

And Max and Charlotte, his children – what about their future? And his tough, burly, obstreperous little grandson, Jack? And the baby growing in Charlotte, swelling her belly with hope? Things would only get worse, for them. The cracks and pits on Gilbert's ceiling, familiar imperfections, were like a road map back to the shadows of his soul, and he traced his route, and journeyed there.

Kitimat

Who was Gilbert Crow? Shoulders hunched, pale skin reflecting her flickering computer screen, Anne found Gilbert Crow in pictures, quotes and sound bites all over the internet. He intrigued her. She found him waving placards at oil pipeline protests in Kitimat, on a bus expedition along the pipeline route, introducing speakers on makeshift stages from the Great Bear Rainforest to the Alberta tar sands. While she cyber-stalked Gilbert Crow, she kept a tab on her browser open to breaking news coverage of the Kitimat oil spill. Volunteers were flocking to Kitimat to help clean up the chemical sludge. Anne couldn't pinpoint the moment she decided to go. She simply found herself packing a bag, and applying to the Churchill Research Centre for emergency leave from her residency.

"What are you doing, Anne? The west coast of this country will respond to the emergency. We need you more than Kitimat does," Ian said, standing in her bedroom doorframe.

"Jane doesn't care if I leave." Anne struggled with the zipper on her suitcase. "Secretly, she'll be overjoyed I'm gone."

Ian opened his mouth then shut it. Jane was holding a grudge about the binoculars incident, for which you couldn't blame her, Anne knew. But still.

"Well, *I'll* miss you."

The zipper on Anne's suitcase wouldn't close. She had overpacked, as usual, but it *was* a shoulder season, and choosing oil-spill-cleanup wardrobe items was tricky.

"Here," said Ian, "let me do that."

"It's fine, really – I've got it."

But Ian's long arms snatched the suitcase from her, and over her protests, he shook the old piece of luggage, urging the zipper closed with violent tugs. The stitching on one side of the zipper disintegrated under this duress and the suitcase split open, spilling its contents of inexpertly folded shirts and pants.

"Sorry, sorry!"

Anne arrived in Kitimat less than a week after the spill, her belongings stuffed in a hiking backpack borrowed from Ian. The propellors of the little plane thundered in her ears as they circled a flat, green valley surrounded by jagged, snow-topped mountains. To the west, she caught glimpses of shimmering blue vistas, the great expanse of the Pacific Ocean. Winding channels from the ocean spread out inland, great marine arteries dividing into veins and capillaries. The landing was bumpy, and Anne felt self-conscious of her extra flesh, shuddering and jiggling.

She descended the aluminum steps and expressed her thanks to the pilot, a handsome man about her age standing proudly on the tarmac, black and gold epaulets jutting out from his broad shoulders. He acknowledged her gratitude with a toothy smile and a wink. Anne felt blood rush to her cheeks and desire throb between her legs. It was dangerous to let years slip by without getting laid, Anne reflected. She flashed the pilot a cheeky smile.

The odour of residual airplane exhaust filled her lungs, reminding her of why she had come. For a crazy second, she thought she was smelling oil from the spill, then she shook her head – Kitimat was fifty-six kilometres to the south of this airstrip. But as she stepped out of the miniature airport and walked toward the lone waiting taxi, Anne couldn't rid her nostrils of the stench of gasoline and chemicals. She frowned, pushing away thoughts of the carbon cost of her trip.

The cab driver was outside his vehicle, leaning on the hood, squishing one tire into the pavement. He was tall and corpulent, dwarfing his taxi, with thick eyeglasses sitting slightly askew on the bridge of his broad nose, and a tag on his shirt that read *Kitimat Kab: Little Ted.* He tossed her heavy bags into the trunk of his cab with practiced nonchalance.

"Where to, the spill? I hope you've got somewhere to stay. Hotels and motels are plugged full of volunteers like you."

"I – no. Do you, do you know Gilbert Crow?"

There was a long pause while Little Ted tilted his head, considering her in his rear-view mirror. He pushed his spectacles up his misshapen nose with a finger, then spoke slowly and deliberately.

"There are just over eight thousand people in Kitimat, and I'm one of three cab drivers. I know everybody. Do *you* know Gilbert Crow?"

"Well, um, no—not exactly. I *feel* that I know him." Anne blundered, and to her amazement, Little Ted didn't laugh.

"You *feel* you know Gilbert. Well, okay. Good enough. Maybe you can help him out."

Little Ted started driving and talking, recapping the last few years in Kitimat, the protests, the highway blockades, the media coverage, and the controversy. There had been activists prophesying environmental disaster, and business magnates touting the pipeline's economic potential. Families had fractured, rent asunder by *yes* or *no,* children turned against their parents.

"Like what happened to Gilbert," said Little Ted. "His daughter Charlotte stood by him against the pipeline, but his son Max liked the sound of the money, and wanted it built. They fought, and it was the last thing those Crows needed. Gilbert's wife Clara had just died of cancer when Elba Energy showed up with their project. Gilbert fought the pipeline with his grief. His friends—like me—we were worried his grief would come, if the pro-pipeline side won. Well, yeah, it did, and Elba Energy built the damn thing. But you know, Gilbert—he was okay. Disappointed, yeah, but okay."

They fell silent. Anne watched the scenery, trees startling in their height, the forest lush and decadent. She had become used to the brown bunch grasses and stunted shrubbery on the shores of Hudson Bay.

"What's your story – you a reporter, or something?"

"Hardly. I'm a biologist. I've been studying polar bears in Churchill, Manitoba."

"So you came because of bears?"

"No. Well, not exactly. I don't know precisely why I'm here. I just need to make a difference right now—somehow. I can't do anything for the polar bears. It's terrible to feel helpless. The ice keeps melting, the bears keep suffering, and I keep gaining weight." Unexpected tears sprang to Anne's eyes. "I don't know why I just said that. I'm sorry. Please excuse me." She wiped her face with her sleeve and looked out the window.

Little Ted stole glances at Anne as he drove. Houses and buildings grew denser. They passed several one-story cheap motels, doors and windows in a row with an office tacked to one end, but every sign said *No Vacancy.* Anne thought she should say something, make light conversation, but it was too late for cheerful small talk. They made a series of turns, terminating on a quiet residential street. Little Ted parked in front of a modest A-frame cabin. He manoeuvred his bulk out of the driver's seat and lumbered around the back of his cab, where he opened the trunk, removed her bags, and carried them over to the wooden porch. Anne got out and followed him tentatively, stopping halfway across the scrubby yard. Her head felt light, as if it were filled with helium. What were they doing here?

"Umm, excuse me, but this doesn't..."

Little Ted didn't seem mentally defective or incompetent, but he had clearly forgotten who she was, and where she wanted to go. Or had she even told him where she wanted to go?

"I was thinking a hotel would be better? Does someone live here?"

Little Ted rapped firmly on the cabin door. There was no answer, and no movement from inside the cabin. The big man turned to face Anne and sighed.

"He's not getting up. We're going to have to just *do* it," said Little Ted, as if it were time to execute a plan they had hatched together. He opened the front door and walked inside, beckoning for Anne to follow him.

"Hey Gil. Yeah, it's Little Ted. You there?" Little Ted waited for a moment and then shouted, "Gilbert! You've got a visitor. She's from Churchill, Manitoba, man."

Gilbert? Was Little Ted going to introduce her? Why had he stopped here – to visit his friend? There was no response from inside the cabin. Anne stood on the threshold, feeling a little panicky, trying to peer around Little Ted for a glimpse of the house's interior. She got an impression of tidiness and good taste in art, wooden masks, bold paintings, and colourful blankets folded neatly over a rocking chair and a couch.

"Listen, I'm here to help clean up the spill," Anne said, as if she had just remembered why she had left her coveted research position and flown across the country on a whim.

Little Ted turned to Anne, his body blocking the entire doorframe of the cabin. He pushed his glasses up the sweaty ramp of his nose, and they immediately slid back down.

"Gilbert hasn't said a word since the spill. He's kinda catatonic in his bedroom, staring at the ceiling. I don't think he's eaten, either. Here's what I think. All that grieving he never got around to – he's doing it now. His kids have been by, but Max is pretty busy at work, and Charlotte's got a rambunctious toddler, and another baby due any day now. She's going to live at her friend's place in Terrace until Kitimat stops reeking. I won't lie, there's still a few rooms for rent in town, but they're crappy. You can sleep on Gilbert's couch for free. You feel you know Gilbert. You don't, but I do, and he's a good man, you're safe here. Any problems, you call me, I'll be here quick."

Little Ted reached two fingers of a huge paw into the breast pocket of his plaid shirt, pulled out a business card, and passed it to Anne.

"You need a ride, call me. There's food in the fridge—Max brought it—and fish in the freezer. Gilbert likes coffee in the morning, and tea for the rest of the day."

The whole thing was strange and sudden. Anne felt like a successful stalker. Was this what she wanted, was this what she had come for? She allowed herself to be guided to Gilbert Crow's beige, overstuffed couch. *It could double as a bed,* she thought. Little Ted brought her backpack inside. He plunked it down heavily beside the couch, pointed meaningfully at a door beside the kitchen, then went and opened it. He spoke to someone inside the room.

"You got a house guest now, Gil. Name's Anne, she likes bears. I'll stop by later, see how you're both getting on." Little Ted drew his bulk out of Gilbert's bedroom and walked past Anne. As he exited the cabin, he turned with an afterthought.

"You should prob'ly make him a cup of tea and a sandwich right away, before he forgets that you're here."

The huge taxi driver pushed up his glasses and smiled, then he was gone.

Highway 16

"Land of the silver birch, home of the beaver, where still the mighty moose wander at will!"

Jonathan was speeding northwest on British Columbia's Highway16 toward Kitimat, belting out old campfire songs. The windows were down on his mother's old blue Volvo wagon, and a pile of camping gear obscured the rear view in the mirror. He sucked in fresh air, and delivered a roadworthy crescendo.

"Blue lake and rocky shore, I will return once more. Boom diddy ah da, boom diddy ah da, boom diddy ah da, boom!"

He sang a series of love songs to no one in particular, his voice warbling with earnest sentiment. He had refuelled in Smithers. It was ten o'clock in the morning on his second day of driving. He was hoping to reach Kitimat well before nightfall and find a decent, free camping spot. He had a cooler full of fruit and cheese, a couple of bags of dry goods, his parents' tent, a camp stove, two sleeping bags, and an air mattress. He also had lots of black clothes. Oil stains wouldn't show up on black.

The spill happened pretty much where everyone was afraid it would – near water. Oil was bleeding right into the Kitimat River. A whole tanker leaking into Hecate Strait would have been worse, but this was bad enough. His social media feed was full of outrage, but there were so many disasters like this these days, people were numb. Even he was inured to pictures of oily birds and scummy water. The last big spill, in the Gulf of Mexico, had sickened the world for a couple of weeks, then it seemed like everyone forgot about it, and went back to business as usual.

Jonathan wondered why he felt peppy and buoyant. This disaster was exactly the kind of thing that he resisted, protested, wrote letters against, signed petitions to prevent, and debated at length in tutorials at his college. Here it was, the real thing, and instead of driving to the scene of a sickening environmental crime, he felt like he was racing toward an opportunity. People would need solutions and expertise, and ta-dah! Here he was, Jonathan Fuhrenmann, almost B.Sc., right around the corner from a degree in environmental sustainability!

Also, he was feeling the high of a spectacular road trip. The highway veered west and then south again. Everywhere around him, jagged black mountains streaked with brilliant patches of snow jutted up into dramatic skies, and every turn brought something sudden and beautiful: a little gem of a lake, a stand of imposing trees, a meadow of late-blooming wildflowers.

"In*tense*," exclaimed Jonathan. It was the mantra for his trip. "In. Tense. Intense. Whoa, man, this is just *in*-fucking-*tense!*"

It was mid afternoon when the blue station wagon rolled into downtown Kitimat with the windows down and the music blasting. His stringy hair was sucked sideways, flapping outside the car. Brilliant sunshine kept his mood aloft, and he wore a hopeful, crooked smile. The epicentre of the oil spill was easy to find. He didn't even have to check his phone for a map. A long line of vehicles bordered a forested area, including two fire trucks and several white trucks that said *Elba Energy* on them in green letters. The spill zone was demarcated with yellow tape screaming CAUTION. Dozens of people—some wearing full hazmat suits—were moving, back in there behind the trees. Jonathan parked, switched out his leather sandals for rubber boots, and strode into the fray.

The stink hit him immediately. His eyes watered and his lungs burned. He squinted toward the workers in the trees, and noted they all wore masks of one kind or another over their mouths and noses. Disconcerted with his lack of foresight, Jonathan returned to his car, extracted a crumpled blue bandana, and fashioned a covering for his face. It would be an inadequate filter, but after driving for two solid days to get here, he was determined to see the spill. He ducked under the yellow tape and made his way toward a knot of people who were struggling with shovels and buckets.

He felt a squishing sensation underfoot, and looked down at the forest floor and his own footsteps behind him. Everything was shiny and black. The whole area was saturated with oil at ground level. Wrinkling his nose, he approached the workers. They were immersing their shovels down into the top layer of vegetation, scooping up crude oil, and depositing it in buckets at a rate of two or three cups per shovelful. It seemed a futile exercise, like scooping up spilled milk with a teaspoon.

"Hey man," Jonathan said. "Is that even going to work?"

A woman stopped and leaned on her shovel. Her black hair was streaked with grey, and her face was lined and grimy.

"Are you even *registered?*"

"Uh, no, man. I, like, just got here."

"White tent. Near the fire engines." She pointed with with a gloved, oily hand. "They'll explain everything to you there."

As he approached the tent, Jonathan saw that it was flanked by four burly police officers. They appraised him as he passed, and he broke out in a nervous sweat. Or maybe he was already toxic from the oil fumes.

Inside the tent, the emergency effort was briskly efficient. Jonathan presented himself at the first wooden folding table, where a woman wrote down his name, driver's license number, and social insurance number.

"Okay. Do you want to work with boom setting, forest skimming, dispersant application, or operating the fire hose?" she asked.

"Umm," said Jonathan. "So, what do you have to do, for those?"

The woman sighed, and recited a memorized spiel.

"Booms need to be secured on the river. They isolate the oil to one spot so it can be vacuumed up. There needs to be a whole series of them between here and the wharf. Boom setting is the cleanest job. Fire hoses are used for pressure-dispersing the oil that's on the riverbanks. You need to be strong, because the pressure is intense. The fire department will show you how to use water pressure to redirect the oil. Forest skimming, you stick a shovel into the puddles on the surface, and scoop the oil into buckets. With chemical dispersants, you need to wear a full hazmat suit and get an hour of training in the tent behind this one." She snapped her chewing gum, waiting for him to decide.

"Uh, boom setting," said Jonathan. He felt like a coward, but those fumes were actually way too much.

"Okay. You'll still need a regulation mask, a suit, and some gloves. You can sign all three out from the tables behind me. Clock in and out every day you work. Return any equipment on your last day, or else you'll get billed for it. Okay?"

"Yeah, okay. Hey, I'm gonna come back tomorrow. I, uh, have to find a camping spot today. Do you know where I can camp?"

She stared at him, her jaw working away at her gum.

"You're on your own. I'm not from here. I'm just here to help with the spill. Next." She craned her neck to see past him, where a queue of volunteers was waiting.

Jonathan stepped aside. He retreated to his car, blinking rapidly. The grim reality of the spill had lowered his buoyant mood. That smell was *horrible.* He somehow hadn't anticipated the omnipresence of it. He would feel better once he got to work setting booms on the water the next day. But before setting out to find a camping spot, he realized that he had another problem. His rubber boots were coated with smears of viscous oil; they would stain anything they came into contact with. He kicked them off without touching them, and rooted around in his vehicle for a plastic bag. He found one, stuffed the boots into it, and placed the bag in the back seat of the Volvo.

He drove back the way he had come, looking for a promising side street or a logging road. The smell of oil was lingering, permeating the car. It was coming from his boots, and the plastic bag was doing nothing to contain it. The fumes were noxious – he could barely drive, his eyes stung and watered. Indignant, he tried to breathe fresh air from his window. Hypothetically, a pipeline rupture was repugnant. In real life, it was heinous, an unpardonable crime!

A dirt road sliced off the highway at an angle on his right. He swerved onto it, and drove until he found a pull out. He parked, got out, and plunged into the forest. Barely twenty steps from the road, he found a flattish clearing. There was no fence, no sign, nothing. It was quiet. No birds sang. Something rustled in the leaves close to where Jonathan stood, startling him. *Oh – a squirrel.* It spiralled up a tree and then froze, its bushy tail wrapped around the trunk, and chittered at him, telling him off.

"Camp spot," he grinned. "It's perfect."

By nightfall, Jonathan was climbing into a cosy cocoon of sleeping bags inside a jaunty electric blue dome tent. His belly was full of boiled veggie dogs, apples, and whole wheat bread. A trampled pathway led from his car, parked up on the road, to his new, rugged, forest domain. He had thrown the bag with his oily rubber boots out of the car. He fell asleep remembering his father's earnest lessons on family camping trips, how to split wood, where to pitch a tent. His old man would be proud of the order his son had imposed on the chaos of this unknown wilderness.

The snuffling and snorting started in his subconscious. In his dream, Jonathan was carrying buckets of scraps and slop to hungry livestock in a farmyard. He was dressed like a cross between a farmer and a clown, in shiny red rubber boots and yellow coveralls. He heaved a bale of hay at a black-and-white Holstein cow that was mooing gently. He fed some chickens grain that appeared magically in his deep pockets; the chickens clucked and pecked cheerfully around his ankles. He fed a donkey, and the beast blinked up gratefully with huge, heavily lashed eyes. But what was he supposed to feed the pig? It was a bright pink pig, a cartoon pig, its tail a perfect spiral. It rooted hungrily with its snout, insistent wet snorting that grew louder and louder. There was nothing to feed it though, and Jonathan went around in circles in his dream-barnyard, chased by the ravenous pig.

Something shoved him, hard, and abruptly he woke up. The wet sniffing didn't end with his dream. The pig was outside his tent, drooling, starving, desperate for food. *There are no pigs in the forest.* But his ears told him there was a big mammal on the other side of the thin fabric between him and the Kitimat night. If it wasn't a pig, it must be...

Jonathan lay stiffly, listening to the bear. He heard a metallic crunch, and remembered how lazily he had wiped his camp stove after boiling his soya bean hot dogs. More metallic scraping, claws or teeth raking along manmade things. More snuffling, more licking, more wet mouth-and-muzzle noises.

He didn't hear the bear approach. Without warning, the tent collapsed at its entrance, pushed down from the outside by the weight of something big and heavy. Pain exploded in his left leg, and he screamed. Claws ripped through the smooth blue nylon, and a huge hairy head pushed into the tent with him. Jonathan's arms scrabbled at his sides, trying to back away from bear, but there was nowhere to go, and it was standing on his leg. *Play dead,* he thought, and he did. Squeezing his eyes shut and lying still, Jonathan waited for the bear to decide his fate.

Afterwards, when he told the story, Jonathan tried to sound casual. *I played dead, man. I mean, what else could I do? I had five hundred pounds of bear on my leg!* The truth was, he had either fainted, or gone into shock. The bear's jaws closed on his left ankle, and he screamed, and the bear pulled him free of the wreckage of his tent.

Outside the tent it wasn't dark anymore, but pale dawn. Some shouts came from up on the road, where Jonathan's car was parked. The bear released Jonathan and stood up, sniffing. Jonathan, coming to, clawed his way into thick ferns and salal. His leg and ankle were hot, wet and sticky with blood.

He found out later that three forestry workers had stopped their truck behind the Volvo to piss in the roadside shrubs. They had heard his screams, shouted back, and scared the bear away, thus saving Jonathan's life.

The bear's forelegs crashed to the ground. It turned and retreated into the forest. In that brief moment, Jonathan saw his attacker in profile. An unmistakeable ragged hump on the bear's upper back confirmed what kind of a bear it was – a grizzly.

The Great Bear Creates Grizzlies

The Great Bear was resting among the stars. She had created the bears, the people, and all the creatures of the earth, and she was pleased. She had not rested for long when she heard squalling and squawking below her.

The Brown Bears of the earth ate well. They harvested berries and nuts, and they ate the fat pink flesh of salmon. They drank clear cold water from rivers and streams. They were so healthy that their cubs grew bigger and stronger with each generation. One spring, all of the mother brown bears gave birth to cubs that were much bigger and stronger than previous brown bears. These cubs quickly realized the advantages of their strength, and they began to bully their own parents, brothers, sisters, and elders.

The salmon run arrived, a great flush of red fish slapping in the river. The big, bullying bears wouldn't let any of the other bears approach the riverbank. The berries turned purple and ripe on the shiny green bushes, and the bullying bears ate all of the fruit themselves. The bears began to argue and fight, disturbing the Great Bear's well-earned rest.

The Great Bear was angry. She sent a drought, which shrivelled the berries. She dried up the salmon streams. The bullying bears didn't share; they were only cubs after all, selfish and immature. The brown bears grew thin, and some died. The survivors wailed and moaned their grief.

The Great Bear reached down with her mouth, as mammals do with their young, and one by one she took the big, bullying bears in her jaws by the scruff of their necks. She shook them vigorously. The big, bullying bears didn't look the same after they had been disciplined by the Great Bear. They were still much bigger than the other bears, but now they also had large tufts of hair on their backs where the Great Bear had grasped them in her jaws.

The Great Bear separated all of these bigger bears and called them Grizzly Bears. The Grizzly Bears were now in direct competition with the brown bears for food. The cubs of the brown bears would never again have so much to eat that they became overgrown bullies. The constellation known as Hercules represents the huge, fierce, ruff-necked Grizzly Bear.

Tlingit

Early, catch two small fish. Eating fish quickly, stomach hurt more after fish, why? Again sky is blue, smooth shore rocks hot on pads of paws. Walking slowly toward the place of many bears. Soon, time to mate. My body says yes, yes, mate again. But the not-thinking of K'ytuk is still strong.

Sensing, sniffing for something to eat. Always, there is the Mountain of Man Things, but where Man Things are, are men also. Danger, beware. Hungry I am, ravenous. Empty, empty Tlingit.

Think of nothing—think nothing. No thinking of danger. Walk slowly, slowly, closer to Man-Thing Mountain. Food-smells fight with man-smells, Tlingit should run away but hungry I am, ravenous. Closing mouth, chew and swallow strangeness. Chew, swallow, survive. I chew, swallow, and survive.

CRACK! I am running away—running and running away. Running and running away!

Kitimat

There was someone in Gilbert's house, a blonde woman with red cheeks and round hips. She had made him a grilled cheese sandwich, opened a can of soda, and she was sitting next to his bed. He was thirsty, so he drank the soda, then rolled onto his back and continued to contemplate the ceiling.

She tried to engage him in conversation, fumbling awkwardly with stock questions, and then blushing in the silences that followed. She seemed kind. She had a wholesome prettiness, like a dairy farm icon.

"Nice place you have here. I really like how you've got it fixed up."

If he answered her, they would keep talking to each other. Soon the chatter would come around to the oil spill, or Clara, or both, and Gilbert wasn't going to talk about those things. So, silence. The blackness had enveloped him.

"Are these pictures of your kids? They look happy. Your daughter – if this is your daughter – she's beautiful."

Charlotte, Charlotte, what kind of world will your babies grow up in?

The blonde woman clucked, an impatient sound. When she spoke again, there was an edge in her voice, like she was tired of humouring him.

"I guess you're upset about the spill. Well, I am too. I left my job in Manitoba. I dropped everything to come here and help."

Anne got Gilbert's attention, briefly, when she mentioned Manitoba. His black eyes flicked over to meet her blue ones. His eyes were flat, dead. It was disconcerting, and Anne turned her head. She was sitting in a clinically depressed guy's bedroom, armed only with a grilled cheese sandwich. She might have left, slung her backpack on her shoulders and walked to find a motel, if he weren't so handsome, so enigmatic. She had been struck by his looks from thousands of kilometres away. In real life, even lying on his bed, mute and brooding, Gilbert Crow was hot. He was the thrilling antithesis of her, long and dark and lean where she was pale, pink and curvy. She was shy to explore him with her eyes at first, but his utter lack of response soon dissolved her inhibitions. She let her eyes travel south of his square chin, down the ropes of his neck to his shirt – oh, it was fastened with only one button, at his waist! The collar was folded open to his shoulders, revealing a smooth, hairless chest and one dark, taut nipple. Anne checked to make sure he wasn't watching her, before going ahead and examining his crotch. Yes, there it was, a bulge in his faded jeans. His legs went on forever; he would be tall, if she could get him off the bed into a vertical position.

She entertained herself by testing the limits of his inattention for a while, then she got bored. Confident he wasn't suffering, and certain that he wasn't going anywhere, she stood up and stretched.

Tentative poking around in Gilbert's cabin soon turned into full-fledged snooping. By mid afternoon, Anne had taken a full inventory of the fridge and larder, familiarized herself with the contents of the various kitchen drawers and cabinets, inspected the bathroom for cleanliness, (quite clean, eight out of ten), and read the spines of all his books, (weakness for legal thrillers, good collection of modern Canadian classics). A self-guided tour of the yard and garden yielded a handful of tough Swiss chard leaves and a few lumpy, misshapen carrots. She checked back on Gilbert every half hour or so. No sign of improvement.

The evening was cool. Anne started a fire in the wood stove, set rice to boil, washed and sliced the carrots, and prepared the salmon for poaching. While the rice was cooking, Anne discovered a wooden box full of photographs jammed on one end of a bookshelf. Investigation gold! She took them out in handfuls, flattened their curled edges, and tried to create a chronology out of the haphazard piles.

She found school pictures—head shots on a blue background—of two handsome children: a girl and a boy. *What had Little Ted said their names were? Charlotte, and Max.* She found fishing pictures of Gilbert and Max, holding up their catches beside a river on a rainy day, their expressions warrior-serious. Here was Gilbert, waving from the half-constructed roof of the A-frame cabin where she sat. And aha! – a faded shot of a couple – Gilbert, and an arrestingly lovely woman with long black braids, full lips, and a physique not unlike Anne's. Gilbert and his wife both wore ceremonial blankets around their shoulders, embroidered with intricate designs, black stylized animals on crimson backgrounds. They were standing under a giant cedar tree, shaggy red bark and swooping green fronds. And here they were in another photo, sitting on the front porch of the cabin, their arms around each other, laughing. There was a series of group shots around the base of a totem pole; Anne wondered if this was Gilbert's extended family. He and Clara were in some of the group photos; they were the youngest people in these pictures.

At the bottom of the box, Anne found another shot of Clara. Her name was scrawled on the back of the picture; otherwise, Anne might not have recognized her. She was leaning against a white pickup truck, frowning. Her curtain of ebony hair was gone, and in its place was a red bandana tied around her evidently naked scalp. She was thin; her cheeks were pale and hollow under high, pointed cheekbones. She looked at the photographer with – what? Loathing? Disgust? Anne guessed Clara hadn't wanted this picture taken.

Anne was holding the photo close to her face, considering it, when the back of her neck tingled and she whirled around, then scrambled to pick up the jumble of photos spread out on the table.

"Oh – you're up!"

Gilbert stared at the open wooden box of pictures on his kitchen table. Anne blushed.

"I'm sorry, I just – made myself at home. I didn't know when you would be getting up, and I was curious, so..."

He went to the stove and turned off the heat under the salmon and the rice. He removed two plates from a cupboard and served the food. Anne hurried to return the photos to their box, her face hot with embarrassment. Gilbert poured two glasses of water, sat down across from her, and took a bite of his dinner. Anne put the wooden box back on the bookshelf and took her place at the table, folding her hands in her lap, knitting her fingers together. Gilbert chewed, swallowed with some difficulty, then took another bite.

"Listen – I don't have to stay here. I don't know why Little Ted brought me here. I'm sure I could find a hotel room. I'll just call a cab and, and be going."

"No," he said, without looking up from his plate. "Stay."

Anne sighed. It would have been a good time to stand up and make a dignified exit. But bottom line, she was hungry.

They ate dinner across from each other. Gilbert managed to avoid her eyes through the whole meal, and neither of them spoke. She had exhausted all her conversational overtures. The lack of interaction got easier between them as the meal went on.

"I'll clean up," Anne offered. She had cooked it, but it was his food, after all. Gilbert nodded, scraped his chair back, and used the table to push himself to his feet. He went back to his bedroom, but he paused in the doorway, and turned to her. Their eyes met, and he smiled, quickly, like the brief flash of a little fish jumping in a flat lake. He went in his room, closing the door softly behind him.

The ripples left behind by his smile kept Anne awake until midnight.

Churchill

Ian nursed his third cup of coffee and surveyed the landscape outside the window, scanning for white specks in motion. His khaki trousers were stained. He had dropped half an egg sandwich on them at breakfast, and couldn't be bothered to change. Without Anne around, he was turning into a sloppy bachelor. Behind him, he heard the busy tapping of Jane's fingers on a keyboard. She wouldn't notice egg on his pants, and if she did, she would consider it bad manners to point it out.

He was thinking about how the work they were doing at the centre affected him. Ian figured he fit in somewhere between Anne and Jane, not as detached and dispassionate as Jane, but nowhere near as sentimental as Anne. If Anne were here, she would be moaning about the soaring mercury in the thermometer, fretting openly about Tlingit, wringing her hands and tearing her hair out. Instead, she was thousands of kilometres away, probably up to her armpits in liquid black poison and freaking out about the oil spill's effects on the wildlife of the Pacific northwest. It must feel good to do something concrete, Ian mused, but Anne had reached Kitimat via a series of carbon-burning aeroplane flights. How did the aphorism go? If you're not part of the solution, you're part of the problem.

Unfolding his crossed legs, Ian's knee bumped the counter and his coffee cup jiggled dangerously beside the computer keyboard. His long arm shot out and snagged the cup, tilting it away from the keyboard, but sloshing a puddle of watery drip-machine coffee onto a pile of graphic statistics he had just generated. *Damn!* He used the edge of his hand to wipe the majority of the spill to the floor, but the papers were ruined – he'd have to reprint them all.

Anne's departure had left an enormous vacuum at the centre, and a sad silence. Her absence wasn't the only source of uneasy feelings wriggling like worms underneath Ian's skin. Jane was tied up in a tighter knot than usual. She was a nucleus of compressed energy, a star about to go supernova. It was weird, because Anne's departure should have eased workplace tensions for Jane. The two women had opposite approaches to just about everything, and they argued almost every day. Jane should have been able to relax without Anne around, but instead, she was seething. Ian stood up to fetch a cloth from the kitchen, and stopped to consider his quiet colleague. Jane's brow was furrowed, and her mouth was pulled sideways into a straight, determined line. *Are those beads of sweat?* It made Ian anxious, just looking at her.

"What's the matter?"

"Nothing." Jane kept typing, and didn't look up. "I'm working, as you can see."

It was bristling like this that drove Anne crazy, but it didn't faze Ian.

"Yes, I can see that. Only, your expression leads me to believe that something's wrong."

Jane paused to glance up at Ian, the furrows on her forehead deep enough to plant onions.

"If you'll excuse me, I want to get this report finished today." She went back to her computer screen.

Ian was dismissed, but he didn't leave right away. He considered the neat part in Jane's short black haircut, a thin white line of scalp. He was close enough to reach out and touch the sleeve of her purple fleece jacket to test the force-field she erected around herself. What would happen if he had had the audacity to reach out and touch her? *ZAP!* A blinding flash of blue-white light! He would be thrown back, violently, against the wall. It wasn't a good time to figure out what was eating Jane Minoto. He would have to wait until she powered down her strong defences.

In the kitchen he ran water in the sink, waiting for it to warm up so he could dampen the ratty, stained rag they were using for a dishcloth these days. He didn't feel like spending the day doing data entry and analysis, neither did he want to hike over dwindling bear habitat. It was as if Anne had left the heavy, itchy cloak of her frustration behind for him to wear. Maybe it was a dump day.

As part of their commitment to the Northern Studies Centre, the scientists performed volunteer work for Churchill's Polar Bear Alert, a program designed to help keep the community safe from polar bear attacks. When he needed a day away from the centre, Ian liked to help scare interested bears away from the municipal garbage dump, and send them back into the wild. He wiped up the spilled coffee, changed his shirt, (best not to smell like an egg sandwich), and grabbed his orange parka, a brown knit toque, and leather mittens.

The Churchill Dump: ignominious location of the best polar bear viewing on the planet. Because the dump was popular with the bears, it also attracted tourists and thrill seekers. It was dangerous, and vaguely embarrassing, and the city was working hard to discourage it. Proper tours for viewing polar bears were established. Bears were scared away from the dump, and the dump itself had been converted into a recycling and waste management facility. The bears still came, though. They were hungry, and the dump was still on their radar as a potential cafeteria. Firing a gunshot or two in the air usually sent the bears loping off toward the shores of Hudson Bay, where slushy ice was already beginning to form. Before white people settled permanently in this area, polar bears in autumn would have rested in day beds—wallows they created in willow thickets or kelp beds along the shore—rising occasionally to test the stability of the ice, shoving it with their massive forelegs. When the ice was thick enough, the bears would venture out on it to hunt for seals. Now humans had permanent settlements where the bears used to live.

Jane didn't acknowledge Ian when he said goodbye. Whatever. It would be good to be away from her anxious energy for a few hours. Ian stopped at the Polar Bear Alert Office, signed out a rifle, and chatted for a few minutes with Frank Hobbes. Frank was a polar bear aficionado, an amateur enthusiast, and an excellent resource for the Northern Studies Centre staff because of his ability to recognize individual bears from a distance.

"We got a new female around the dump. Real skinny and skittish. Wouldn't get too close if I were you. She looks like she'd pick fight over flight. I'm thinking she needs a permanent move up to Wager Bay, before she gets to be a problem. Better take a tranq dart gun with you just in case."

Ian nodded, and accepted the equipment Frank handed him. They discussed the weather, *hot as blazes, pond hockey season's gonna be late,* then Ian drove to the waste management building.

The air was crisp. It wasn't quite cold enough to freeze the garbage solid and suppress the smell. Ian wrinkled his nose, adjusting to the reek of rotting meat and used diapers. Peering through his binoculars, he counted four bears and three tourists. First things first – get the gawkers out of here. Usually the sight of Ian and his gun, coupled with a warning, was enough to make tourists leave. On this day, the tourists were hardy Europeans, three men in their sixties. The sight of Ian and his gun approaching didn't faze them.

"Hi guys! Hey, there's four polar bears a little too close to here for comfort. Going to have to ask you to clear the area," said Ian amiably.

"Zey are not eenterested een us," one of the tourists said, shrugging.

"Not yet, they aren't. If they *do* get interested, they won't be coming over to shake your hand." Ian patted the rifle.

"We take ze photographs, zen we go," the tallest tourist replied, indicating his large professional camera. The other two men were taking iPad videos of the bears, holding their devices high, fiddling with zoom functions.

Ian glanced nervously at the group of bears. The animals had stopped milling around the big garage doors of the waste management building, and were standing stock-still, staring at the humans.

"Listen, those bears can outrun deer. If they decide to charge, they'll get here before you guys can run away."

Among the bears was a smallish individual, the skinny one Frank had mentioned. Ian lifted his binoculars again. Unless he was mistaken, the new-to-civilization bear was none other than Tlingit! She had a lopsided look to her muzzle, and there was that smudge of greyish skin near her nose, probably a scar from a fight. It was Tlingit, all right, and though she was far away, Ian thought he could feel the bear's tension.

"Gentlemen, I'm going to *insist* you return to your vehicle at this point. I'm going to fire this gun overhead, and I can't predict which way those bears will run."

Loudly, obviously, Ian took the safety off of the gun.

The shortest man, a plump fellow with a salt-and-pepper beard, inserted a hand into the front pocket of his puffy, blue down parka. He pulled out a half-eaten granola bar, peeled the foil wrapper back, and took a leisurely bite, gazing pleasantly at the white carnivores, now only the length of a parking lot away from him.

"What? No, you don't—" Ian stopped short.

It was too late. Tlingit had caught the scent of something edible, or the sense of something threatening. She charged.

Ian reacted by immediately firing two gunshots into the air. The other three bears turned on their heavy haunches and ran from the dump back toward the water, rumps rippling, tails bobbing. The charging bear stopped in her tracks.

Going for a kill shot was risky. If Ian shot her now, and didn't shoot her cleanly, there was only a chance he would have time for a second or third try. He was a clumsy guy, but a decent marksman, and he could probably kill her, but Ian really didn't want to put a bullet in *any* polar bear. Especially not Anne's beloved bear. He switched weapons, shouldered the tranquilizer gun, took aim, and fired it into the bear's shoulder. The bear registered the pain, shaking her narrow head. Then, bad luck – she resumed her charge.

From a holster on his chest, Ian grabbed his canister of bear spray. He braced himself. The life-or-death aspect of polar bear watching finally clicked with the tourists, and he heard them screaming and running away behind him, their boots thudding on packed dirt and gravel. He felt strangely calm. Training had taught him his best chance of survival was a well-aimed blast of bear spray, not a bullet. A tranq dart was already embedded in the bear's flesh, but she thundered toward Ian with murderous intent. He pulled the pin on the spray canister. Ten meters from him, she put on the brakes, skidding to a muddy stop. She sniffed in his direction, her top black lip sneering, pulled back, exposing sharp yellow teeth.

He never had to spray her. The anaesthetic in the dart kicked in. Confused, she slung her head sideways, and bit at the dart on her shoulder. Ian dug in, spray canister ready. She chewed at her shoulder for a long minute, glancing at him slowly, then slower still. She began to roll her head from side to side, trying to focus. She collapsed, and a warm wave of relief washed through Ian's body, like a long-held stream of urine. He pressed the talk button on his two-way radio.

"Bear down, Frank. South side of the waste building. I need restraining straps and tranq antidote. Do you copy?"

Ian heard something high-pitched in his own voice, a vestige of fear, and remembered the shrieking European tourists. He scanned the parking lot and found them, watching the drama unfold from the perceived safety of their rented pickup truck, eating granola bars.

Beep bleep. Frank's scratchy reply came over the radio.

"Roger, Ian. Ten-four. Proceeding to your location immediately. Our ETA is seven minutes."

I tranquilized Tlingit. Anne's not going to like this.

Gilbert and The Great Bear

The peaks and valleys, lines and smudges on Gilbert's bedroom ceiling led him into sleep, into a land of dreams.

He is walking in darkness, his senses tingling. Tiny pinpoints of light surround him, overhead and underfoot. The lights are stars, and he is glittering, too. His movement scatters beams of light into a black, opaque void. Gravity is altered here; his body is suspended, almost weightless. There is no forward or backward, but he moves onward, taking slow steps and deep breaths. This atmosphere has a pleasant coolness, it caresses his skin. *I am naked,* Gilbert thinks. He is naked.

In the distance, another people-star sways, moving in his direction, walking with the same slow, steady steps he takes. The star's gait matches his exactly. It's as though he's walking toward a mirror, until the star gets close enough for him to see she is a woman, and she is also naked. Her full, dark breasts bounce gently with the rhythm of her paces. She is illuminated from the inside. Closer still, he makes out her long, dark hair, the smooth curve of her belly, and her smile, a little bit lopsided. She is beautiful and familiar. She is Clara.

To see her again – oh, how he wants to hold her! He opens his arms and waits for his Clara to come into his embrace, to press her full softness against his cool, flat chest. But she stops before she reaches him, and shakes her head mournfully. Gilbert lets his arms fall empty to his sides. From nowhere, a massive bear lumbers up next to her. She places a hand on the bear's side, underneath the beast's shaggy left shoulder.

He has missed Clara desperately, but when he looks at the bear, its eyes catch his, and he cannot tear his gaze away. The bear's coat shimmers, changing from yellow to black to white to cinnamon. It's not a bear Gilbert recognizes, and at the same time, it's every bear he has ever seen, or heard of, or read about. Abruptly he knows who She is, and he understands her. She is the Great Bear, the female mother of all bears, and he cannot touch her the way Clara does, because he is still alive. Clara sways in his peripheral vision, but the Great Bear holds his attention, holds it like his focus is a fish trapped in her jaws.

She changes, and becomes Moksgm'ol, the Spirit bear. Gilbert gasps. This incarnation of Moksgm'ol is desperate and terrified. Gilbert feels hunted and afraid for himself, as if he is being pursued by killers. The beleaguered bear raises one giant paw, its creamy fur marred with a tarry substance.

The Great Bear releases her hold on Gilbert's attention. Clara is crying, one of her hands still twisted in the bear's fur.

Moksgm'ol

I run beyond the range of mere men. Moksgm'ol can climb where men cannot. Instinct and rage have brought me to a dark cool place. Snow is near. The air has the crispness and bite of frost, and it carries scents of cedar and spruce. Cool rocks, wet moss. I know this grove. It is far above valley bottom, a place of quiet creeks, of caves and silence. Mother of Moksgm'ol brought me here as a cub. She taught me well where I might hide when men encroach.

I stop running. I have left men far beneath me, but a distressing odour clings to my nostrils. It comes from my own paws. There is something on my paws that stinks of men. Now that I have stopped, I feel a stinging on the pads of my paws, and I want to assuage it with my tongue. I feel that I should not do this, yet the stinging must be soothed. I lick the blackness on my left forepaw, and then my mouth burns with the taste of death!

Moksgm'ol is too far from rivers to drink cool water! I lick the leaves of the shrubs, the bark of trees. My throat is burning and my paws stink, man has defiled Moksgm'ol! What manner of man's madness is this?

I hear my own whimpering, the squeaking cries of a creature besieged, as when I was a soft, stumbling cub. For shame! For shame!

I run again, crash over and through. I stop in a clearing and shake my head from side to side, trying—oh trying—to escape the infernal fumes attached to this blackness that is attached to me, to Moksgm'ol!

I must climb as far as the snowline to find relief, though now is the Time of the Valley Bottom. Man has pushed Moksgm'ol out to the coldness and purity of high places, of rock and snow, to purge his poisons.

Kitimat

Anne opened her eyes shortly after dawn and unfolded her cramped, stiff limbs from the confines of the couch. A chorus of birds chirped and sang outside the cabin. She was disoriented. Sitting heavily, tousling her hair with dazed fingers, she remembered there was a depressed man in the next room, and she was supposed to help him. What if he was suicidal? God, why hadn't she thought of that? A grunt from the bedroom relaxed her. Phew, he hadn't offed himself in the night.

She found coffee, paper filters, a loaf of bread, and a basket full of apples. Barefoot, she stood on the broad wooden plank floor and made breakfast, stripes of gold autumn sun slanting in, dust dancing where they lit up the room. How best to cheer up Gilbert Crow? Anne had some unorthodox, inappropriate ideas. Fear that her methods might backfire kept her from opening the bedroom door and carrying out an experiment or two.

She was buttering toast when the door opened on its own, and he emerged.

"I had a dream last night about a bear."

Gilbert padded into the kitchen, giving her the briefest of nods as he passed. He had skipped over the courtesy of a morning salutation, and Anne was tongue-tied. He wore a pair of cut-off shorts, nothing else. The little wood stove had kept the cabin warm overnight, but still. He should really put something else on. Or take something off, and go back to bed, with her. Where was she supposed to look? He puttered in the kitchen, wiping the counter. Anne decided to feign nonchalance.

"A bear dream, eh? So, what happened?"

"My wife, Clara, was in the dream too, and now that I think about it, it was *two* bears. You know, Clara – you were looking at her pictures last night."

Anne blushed.

"One was a Spirit bear. It had oil on its paws. I think the other one, the big one, was the Great Bear."

"The Great Bear?"

"Stories." Gilbert waved a hand. "Stories my family told me. Hey, I'm sorry, but what did you say your name was?"

"I didn't. I'm Anne, Anne McCraig. I am so sorry – I never even introduced myself. You're Gilbert. I'm afraid I had an unfair advantage."

Anne stood up and extended a formal hand toward her host. He took her hand gently and unconventionally, between both of his. It was a tender, intimate gesture. Anne almost yanked her hand away out of modesty, but instead she sucked in a deep breath and met his eyes, deep black pools, appraising her. They weren't flat or despairing, the eyes of an unhappy person, at all – in fact, there was a distinct twinkle in them. She pulled her hand back, and wiped her sweaty palm on her pyjama pants.

"Listen, you don't have to put me up, you know. Yesterday I was tired, and kind of overwhelmed. I can easily get a hotel -"

"If you want," Gilbert shrugged. "I thought you wanted to help with the spill. I'm going to find that bear, the one with the oily paws."

"The one from your *dream*?"

"Why not?"

"Um, because it was just a dream?"

Anne buttered more toast and passed a plate to Gilbert. He sat down across the table from her and took an enthusiastic bite. Crumbs fell to the plate and table, and unselfconsciously he wiped them into a broad palm.

"Mmmm, doesn't mean there aren't animals that need our help. The bear was symbolic, maybe. Anyway, should we go and try? You don't look convinced."

"I was going to go to– you know, the official cleanup. I was going to volunteer for that. I mean, I am going to."

"Oh. I thought you were going to help *me,*" Gilbert said, his face serious.

The situation was slipping away from Anne, like slippery rope through damp hands.

"Okay, one, I hardly know you. And two, according to Little Ted, you're supposed to be in some kind of grief-induced coma."

Gilbert put an entire triangle of toast into his mouth, chewed, and swallowed before answering.

"One, you know me well enough to move into my house, and go through my stuff while I'm sleeping. And two, you don't know Little Ted. He's the worst kind of matchmaking busybody you can imagine. Little Ted would hook your grandmother up with the Big Bad Wolf. And dream or no dream, I'm going to see what I can do to help with the cleanup effort. But I'm going to do it my own way, Elba Energy be damned. You caught me at a bad time. I bottomed out yesterday. But today... I have to move forward. I have a grandson. And another grandchild on the way."

Amazing, what people do for their kids. A desire for children of her own clutched at Anne, for little people she had made, whose uncertain future on the warming planet she could fret over. Unbidden, the memory of Tlingit crying for her drowned cub on the shore of Hudson Bay came to Anne, and tears pricked the corners of her eyes.

"I was so upset about the spill – I came out here on impulse. I can't think why I agreed to stay here with you. I've a good mind to call up Little Ted, and invite myself over to sleep on *his* couch."

"Don't do that," said Gilbert quickly. "You really *are* welcome here. Little Ted interferes, but he means well. I had the blues, and you helped snap me out of them. What did you say you do, where you're from? Wherever that is?"

"I didn't." Anne sniffed, and dabbed at her eyes with her sleeve. "I'm a scientist, a researcher. I have an internship at the Churchill Northern Studies Centre, in Manitoba. I'm studying the effects of climate change on the polar bear population there."

"Whoa. A bear specialist – no kidding!"

"Yes, well. Polar bears. Mostly we count them. Tell me more about the Great Bear stories."

Gilbert stood and stretched, extending long arms toward the ceiling. He closed his eyes and yawned. His hair was so long it brushed the denim waistband of his shorts.

"I'm not a great storyteller. You should hear the Great Bear stories from someone who's good, like my daughter Charlotte. Hey, I'm going to get dressed. Then let's go see how bad things are."

"Alright" Anne said. She tucked errant strands of hair behind her ears, and smoothed the back of her head with a self-conscious hand, aware of the pinking of her cheeks.

A quarter of an hour later, Anne had her first glimpse of the severity of the spill. A spacious white volunteer tent, something you might rent for a rainy-day wedding reception, Anne thought, was abuzz with activity when she and Gilbert entered. People were lined up three and four deep in front of folding tables, signing their names on clipboards, and accepting face masks and gloves. Then someone recognized Gilbert.

Loud conversations became hushed and whispered, and a few people pointed in their direction, then quickly averted their eyes. Anne heard Gilbert's name muttered here and there. Beside her, he sighed heavily.

"I was a spearhead in the pipeline resistance," Gilbert said quietly, so only she could hear. "I think they're expecting a tantrum."

After a few moments, activity in the tent resumed. Several people at once approached Gilbert, and then he was caught up in private conversations. Feeling superfluous, Anne wandered outside the tent and peered into the forest.

The lush green vegetation, towering trees, and chlorophyll-dense undergrowth were a world away from the flat, scrubby shores of Hudson Bay. Cedar branches swooped down gracefully, elegant, like formal arms extended, invitations to a timberland dance. Sprays of fern in the undergrowth were outsized, Mesozoic. Moss grew on everything, rocks and tree trunks. Even the cement curb of the parking lot beside the tent had caterpillars of moss creeping along its cracks. Anne rolled her eyes backward, then tilted her head, trying to take in the height of Sitka spruce with a meters-thick trunk, and got dizzy with the effort.

Soon she saw past the rainforest fairyland, into the sinister trouble that up until now she had only smelled. Thick articulated plastic hoses snaked through wet leaves and mud. One end of each hose was attached to a suction truck, and there were half a dozen of these vehicles, engines whining, diesel pumps rumbling. Bodies in day-glo orange vests toiled in the trees, some straining to carry white buckets, their rims stained with telltale shiny black sludge. Even through a paper mask she slid over her mouth and nose, the fumes assaulted Anne, searing her lungs.

Then Gilbert was beside her, and he spoke without preamble.

"Spirit Bear. Seen running north from here, first day of the spill. My friend Gary, he's a pilot, he can do a fly-over tomorrow. See if we can spot it along the river. It's the bear from my dream."

Anne raised a skeptical eyebrow, but Gilbert had already turned and started down a path of fresh wood chips leading to the riverbank. Anne trailed along behind him, her feet squelching underneath her in the muck. They passed volunteers shovelling up oily wood chips and spreading fresh ones, their masks obscuring their expressions. Anne thought she felt a grim atmosphere of resignation.

The river winked at them through the trees, flashing blue and white where sun glanced off the water. The trees thinned, the ground underfoot changed from damp springy forest floor to round river rock. Anne gasped. An open view of the river made it possible to see the enormity of the task. Pools of black liquid had formed in every low spot, every drainage, and every hollow on the riverbank. The oil took the sunlight and split it into macabre, inky rainbows. Dazed, she walked with Gilbert out into the open, where people armed with hoses and buckets were lifting rocks, one by one, and rinsing the oil off of them. *One at a time,* Anne thought, *rock by rock.* They dropped clean rocks into buckets, and behind them came more volunteers with larger hoses who pressure-washed the shore, diverting the oil into plastic-lined pits that yet more volunteers had dug with shovels.

Anne and Gilbert squinted into the low, powerful sun. Anne made out two lines of boats, one heading upriver and the other down. At first she was relieved to see booms in place, stretching from the south bank to the north bank, both east and west of where she and Gilbert stood. The spill's infiltration of the previously clean, pristine Kitimat River seemed limited and contained. Somehow this illusion bolstered her spirits, and with renewed determination she obtained buckets and hoses for herself and Gilbert. They joined the rock-washers. No one spoke. Anne snuck a glance at Gilbert. His face betrayed nothing.

Shouts rang out from the boats occasionally, but Anne and Gilbert focused on the oily rocks onshore. Close to noon, Anne heard a strangled yell from out on the river. She followed the sound to a man who was leaning over the gunwales of a small aluminum boat. He held a netted fish out over the water. The fish wasn't thrashing. It was still, its scales and gills choked with viscous black mucous. Tears sprang to her eyes, and she turned her head.

But Gilbert passed his bucket and hose to another volunteer, and walked to the water's edge, where he stood ramrod-straight, his long black ponytail drifting eastward in the breeze. Anne abandoned her cleanup tools and joined him there. He didn't acknowledge her, but began to speak.

"My mother washed me and my sisters in these waters. We collected berries with my grandmother and rinsed them in the river not far from here. I caught my first fish upriver a ways, and my father and grandfather taught me how to clean it, and we washed the blood off our knives, and the blood mixed with the water. My father and I fished this river many times after that, and he told me the stories of my ancestors. Clara and I brought Charlotte and Max to the river almost every day, and we passed those stories on to our children."

Anne's tears coursed freely. She wiped them away with her sleeve.

A bald eagle flew overhead and released its piercing keen. They both followed its flight until it came to rest, heavily, on the upper branch of a tree overhanging over the river. The eagle rotated his white head imperiously, frowning, surveying this strange invasion of his fishing grounds. The bird cried again, opening sharp curves of his great yellow beak.

"I'll tell you a story," said Gilbert.

The Great Bear Gives Eagle his Cry

The bears were proud of their place in the circle of life. Smaller creatures bowed before their terrible majesty, then scuttled away in awe and fear. The bears began to think they were superior to all of the other creatures of the earth. But one creature's existence troubled them, and threatened their place at the pinnacle of creation – Eagle.

The bears were jealous Eagle could fly. When salmon were scarce, the bears saw Eagle fly out over the water and catch big, juicy salmon that were unreachable from shore. Again and again Eagle would swoop down make a kill before a bear could swat the same fish, or steal food right out from under a bear's muzzle. After a time, the Bears became so envious of Eagle that they began to complain.

Eagle is the Great Bear's messenger, and the Great Bear created Eagle to be strong and swift. It was Eagle who informed the Great Bear that the bears were jealous of flight, and bemoaned their landlocked existence. But the Great Bear only laughed.

Eagle encouraged all the eagles to provoke the bears. On silent, soaring wings, eagles swooped down and startled the bears. They spotted bears stalking fish in the river, timed their deadly dives perfectly, and stole fish after fish from the frustrated, enraged bears. Not content with the bears' roars, the eagles flew to nearby branches and ate their fish in full view, out of the bears' reach. The bears roared their displeasure toward the sky, and the Great Bear heard them.

The Great Bear had given Eagle the gift of a silent approach, to make the king of wing-borne creatures more lethal. She called Eagle to her.

"You have the mightiest wings, the most savage beak and claws, and the clearest and sharpest vision of any of the creatures of the air. Now I am going to give you a unique and loud cry, and I am going to compel you to use it. All of the creatures on the surface of the earth will know when Eagle is near."

Eagle's beak opened. A loud, high-pitched call rang out, and the sound of it carried over mountains, into valleys, along riverbeds and across ocean inlets. The bears heard the call, and knew that Eagle was nearby. Then the bears were once again content with their place in the world.

Moksgm'ol

This infernal slick blackness cannot be purged from the paws of the mighty Moksgm'ol! My polluted paws have fouled the cold white snow, yet the blackness and the reek remain. Again and again I have passed my muzzle against the poison and attempted to remove it. My eyes smart and weep, and my nose burns. I am angry. I roar with displeasure.

O Man, your noises despoil the rustle and hum of the forest. The lapping and gurgling of the waters are drowned by your ugly sounds. O Man, your hard grey roads bring flashes of speeding light and sudden, gruesome death.

O Man! O Man, your machines rip down the trees that are my home, the forest which has for all time been Moksgm'ol's sanctuary and birthright.

O Man, you tear away the berry bushes. You destroy the soft fruits of the undergrowth, you leave us wandering, hungry.

O Man, what manner of madness is this vile toxin that stains the purity of paws, sears tongue and throat and nose, a poison spreading in sinister silence in Moksgm'ol's home?

I retreat to the safety of the farthest place, robbed of my crown. Even sleep has been stolen from Moksgm'ol. I cannot distance my ruined fore-paws from my beleaguered muzzle.

Kitimat Health Centre

"Yeah, I'm lucky, I know."

Jonathan was irritable. His tone was scratchy and impatient. The smile faded from the glossy pink lips of the pretty young nurse who had come to check the bandages on his thigh.

"Doesn't *seem* like it," said the nurse. She pressed a dressing down firmly onto his left thigh and briskly taped it in place, then wordlessly checked his vital signs, and disappeared through the opening in the green curtains.

Jonathan wanted to call her back and explain. Everyone was telling him how lucky he was. *I thought I'd seen it all - you're the luckiest son of a bitch I've ever met,* the emergency room doctor had said. Then a reporter and photographer from the local newspaper had come to his bedside. *So you just decided to pitch your tent in some random place in the forest—in grizzly bear country? Man, you're lucky to be alive.* Even his mother told him how lucky he was, screeching into the telephone. *Punctures, scratches, and bruises - that's all? My God, Jonathan, you lead a charmed life. You gave me a heart attack, do you realize that?*

He peeled up the tape and lifted the bandage the nurse had just replaced. Underneath were four long lacerations, a row of black stitches in each of them. His thigh was puffy, stained yellow and green between each claw mark. He observed it, detached from the piece of meat that used to be his leg. It was bruised and traumatized, the doctor had said, but as long as there was no infection, he'd heal, and then enjoy showing off his scars and telling his survival story. *Like that was going to happen.* His left ankle was taped up with bandages too, but the twenty-eight puncture wounds and purple bruising down there were too hard for him to examine.

"Walking will be slow and painful for two or three weeks, but just remember how lucky you are." The doctor had pronounced, shaking his head. "Usually grizzlies go for the head and neck. It would have been game over then. Or at the very least, mutilation. Disfigurement."

The Kitimat Health Centre emergency room was swamped, Jonathan learned, eavesdropping through the sage green curtains drawn around his bed. He was surrounded by people suffering from inhalation of oil fumes. The cleanup crew was supposed to wear breathing protection, but clearly the flimsy masks they were handing out in the volunteer tent weren't working.

Jonathan was released three days after he was admitted. He told the doctor who discharged him he planned to join the oil spill cleanup crew immediately. She shook her head.

"Bad idea. You risk opening up and infecting those wounds. You won't be able to spend all day standing or walking. You should go home. Heal up. There's no shortage of volunteers."

"No, I'm staying. There's got to be something I can do." He hadn't driven all the way up the coast to turn around again and rush home. He imagined telling his friends, or his professors at the college, how he had never even made it to the spill site.

A nurse, not the young, pretty one but an older, sensible-looking woman with short grey hair, stood beside the doctor.

"So, where are you going to live? The paramedics said your tent is toast."

Jonathan blinked. His thoughts were fuzzy from painkillers. He hadn't even thought about his tent, likely lying in ribbons right where he had staked it. Imagining the remains of his tent brought back the images of bear claws ripping through blue nylon, an enormous wet muzzle, and a shaggy monster. Blood drained from his head, and he sank back onto the bed.

"Go home and take care of yourself, Jonathan," said the nurse. She placed a folded pair of pale blue hospital pyjama pants on his legs. "You can keep these, if you want. The track pants you were wearing were destroyed. Do you want me to call you a cab?"

A cab. Where would he ask the cab driver to take him? The Volvo was still parked on the road above his campsite. The keys to his car were stashed on top of the rear passenger tire. The thought of returning to the scene of the attack made his stomach clench with fear.

"A cab, um, sure," said Jonathan. "Um, has anyone seen—I mean, does anyone happen to know where the, um, bear is?"

The doctor smiled wryly.

"We've got a situation on our hands here in Kitimat, as you know. I don't think the police, or conservation officers, have been able to track your grizzly. It was nice to meet you, Jonathan. I'd wish you good luck, but you already have loads of the stuff!" She shook Jonathan's hand.

"Cab's on the way," said the nurse.

Slowly, gently, Jonathan eased the soft blue pyjama pants over his tender legs and hobbled toward the hospital exit. Brilliant fall sunshine poured in through the tall glass doors, which slid open at his approach. Outside, Jonathan blinked and peered in both directions for his taxi. Directly in front of the exit stood a mountain of a man, tall and broad, a gloss of sweat on his corpulent face. He pushed a pair of dark-rimmed prescription glasses up his nose, unfolded a thick arm, and waved a hand as big as a pork roast. He was leaning on, and almost obscuring, a beat-up burgundy sedan.

"Hey. You the guy who needs a cab?"

* * *

Beads of perspiration collected on Jonathan's forehead, and his armpits were slick with sweat. Whistling a cheerful melody, Little Ted pulled his taxicab up beside Jonathan's abandoned car. Trees loomed over the road. It was a clear day, but under the thick forest canopy there was darkness, a trickery of shadow and light. Jonathan's aches and pains flared up. The drugs must be wearing off, he thought, and he wondered if he had been too impulsive, leaving the hospital so soon. At least this hulking cab driver was interested and concerned, and hadn't yet told him how lucky he was, which was refreshing. No snickering or hind-sight bear-attack advice.

"So, I guess you need a motel room now, eh? Unless you brought a spare tent."

Jonathan gulped. He scrambled to invent some options, mentally shuffling through his thin hand of cards. He could drive back down to Vancouver, retreat dishonourably with his tail between his legs, a frightened and defeated squirrel. This was his least favourite option. He could afford another tent, but he was too chicken to get out of the cab and walk a few meters to the Volvo, so where would he find the nerve to camp? Renting a cheap motel room would mean borrowing money, and there he knew he was out of luck.

Little Ted parked his cab and turned it off. The windows were rolled down. Birds rustled in the undergrowth. A soft whisper of wind rustled through high branches. Seconds ticked by, a minute. Jonathan stared out at the unbridgeable gulf between the two vehicles. There was a heap of fabric stuffed under the driver's door of the Volvo – the remains of his tent and bedding, Jonathan guessed, thoughtfully stashed by the forestry workers who had scared the bear away.

Little Ted whistled his happy tune, mischief hidden behind the thick lenses of his glasses. Jonathan sighed.

"Guess no one has seen that bear."

"No," Jonathan said, a glum little syllable.

"Could still be around then."

"Mm-hmm."

"You got your keys on you?"

"Uh, no." said Jonathan. "They're on top of the rear passenger tire."

Silence. More birds rustling, another gust of wind.

"I'll go see if they're still there," offered Little Ted.

Jonathan opened his mouth to object, then he closed it. His injuries smarted; the pain was really kicking in here, near the attack scene. Little Ted stuffed a leg-sized arm down beside his bulk and found the door handle. He lumbered out of the cab, leaving his door open. A tinny pinging alarm sounded, comforting Jonathan. It was a human sound, strange enough to scare away any interested fauna – deer and raccoons, and such. Jonathan found he couldn't turn his head to watch Little Ted's progress, but sat tense and immobile, listening first to heavy steps, then to fumbling around, and car doors opening and closing. Finally he heard the rough, rumbling ignition of the Volvo.

"She started up, no problem," announced Little Ted, as if Jonathan's difficulty proceeding to his own car had been a mechanical issue. "Why don't you get in there, and follow me?"

"Uh, where are we going?"

"There's a place you can crash for a couple of days, until you feel better. My friend's place. He likes interesting company."

"For free?"

"In a manner of speaking. For interesting company. Also, you should probably cook and do dishes."

"Okay," said Jonathan.

Gingerly Jonathan climbed out of the cab, stumbled over to the shuddering Volvo, and got behind the wheel. Little Ted had stuffed the wrecked camping gear in the back seat. As they drove back to Kitimat, Jonathan realized he'd never told Little Ted what his intentions were. How had the cab driver known he wanted to stay in town?

They drove to a tidy A-frame log cabin. Little Ted climbed the steps to the front door, Jonathan heard the stairs creak and saw them bend underneath the man's weight. The cab driver opened the cabin door without knocking, peered inside for a moment, then called back to Jonathan.

"Yep, you can stay here. This is my friend Gilbert's place. Tell him Little Ted brought you here. He's got someone else from out of town staying on his couch, but you still have a bedroll and a pillow, right?"

"Are you sure, man?" Jonathan was already out of his car, extracting his damaged sleeping bag, dirt-and-needle encrusted foam mattress, and wrinkled pillow from the back seat.

"Yeah, it's cool. Cook up something for dinner if you can. There's plenty of groceries. If you need a ride, or it doesn't work out, here's my card."

Little Ted returned to his taxicab and sat inside it, fiddling with his cell phone. Jonathan limped to the cabin, let himself in, and made himself at home.

Yukuai

Something is different today, but it is not a good or an interesting different thing. This morning it is agonizing to move. I wake on my side underneath the hard shelter. Lumps of pain inside my skin have become fireballs. I roll, brace my weight on cold walls of man, somehow push to standing. I will my legs to carry me to the fence place for feeding. When the noisy, rolling man-thing comes with bamboo, however, I find that I cannot move toward the crunchy green food, and I find that I do not care. The bamboo-throwing man doesn't notice my lethargy.

The crowds arrive. My vision is blurry; the people are a moving smear of unnatural colour. The crowds bring their usual cacophony and fetid odours, but I am immobile. I am trying to be invisible. I am trying to disappear.

"Mommy what's wrong with the panda?"

"Beats me, Charlie. He looks depressed. Brian, hey Brian! Come look at this panda!"

"This sign says that bear's name isYoo Koo Eye, and it's Chinese for happy! That's so funny, this is the saddest bear I've ever seen!"

I hear the voice of a woman I have smelled, a she-man I know. She is kind, she speaks to me often in the evening, after the throngs of men are gone.

"Happy, how are you?"

"Hey, do you work here?" Harsh man sound. "What the hell is wrong with your panda?"

I cannot move. I remain upright, the lumps of pain within me are searing live coals. It is as though I have eaten fire.

"This is bull crap. Come on, Wanda. It's just some panda, it doesn't even move – it even looks like a fake. Your panda looks fake!"

Now my forelegs can no longer support my weight. They buckle underneath me. My head and chest hit the grey man-ground. The impact and the momentum topple me entirely, and I fall. Excruciating pain of fire licks at me from the inside of my body.

Then there are men – here – inside my enclosure. I sense them, and all of my instinct and experience screams at me to attack, attack, gain freedom! I want to harm them before they harm me, for there is always harm when they come near. My brain fires signals, but my limbs only twitch in response.

"He's still moving. Get out the dart gun. We can't take any chances."

There is a sharp report, and a tiny sting of pain, and then blissful, merciful oblivion.

Kitimat

"Hi, I'm Jonathan. Uh, Little Ted said I could stay here, so I just put my stuff over there beside the bookshelf, okay? I made a salad, and some grilled cheese sandwiches. Your garden is sweet, by the way."

There was a lanky young white man in Gilbert's cabin, talking to Anne about the garden and assuming it was hers. The kid – he couldn't be more than twenty-five, Gilbert guessed – was wearing blue hospital pyjama bottoms and a white plastic inpatient bracelet. It occurred to Gilbert that Little Ted wasn't dropping wandering, confused misfits on his doorstep for their benefit alone. Gilbert crossed his fingers, hoping this kid wasn't a psych patient.

"It's *my* garden, this is *my* place. I'm Gilbert Crow. This is Anne, she's visiting from out east."

"Oh, sorry, man. Well, cool setup you've got here."

Jonathan smiled, a facial contortion that ended as a wince.

"Are you hurt?" Anne asked.

"Um, kind of. Okay I'm just going to spit it out, I got mauled by a bear a few nights ago. I was camping, and the bear wrecked my tent. I came from Vancouver to help clean up the oil spill."

"You *what?* Oh my goodness, you should sit down. Here, I'll push my blankets out of the way."

Gilbert watched Anne rearrange her bedding on his sofa to make room for his new house guest. She hastened to take over in the kitchen, serving the salad and sandwiches onto plates, squirting a dollop of ketchup onto each. If Clara were alive, she would have done the same thing, he thought, and rushed to mother a gawky, awkward loner.

A day of washing rocks and hauling buckets of oily sand had left Anne and Gilbert ravenous. They fell on the meal gratefully, prodding Jonathan to back up and tell his bear attack story from the beginning. Jonathan picked at a sandwich while he spoke, and when he got to the part where the bear clawed his thigh, he pushed his plate away and turned a pale, sickly green.

"You need to sleep," said Gilbert.

Jonathan nodded and tottered unsteadily to his makeshift bed on the floor. He stretched out, and fell asleep within minutes.

"Poor thing," Anne whispered, pushing out a plump lower lip.

"Nah," said Gilbert. "He's lucky. Come on, let's go sit on the front porch and watch the sun set."

They settled politely on either end of a rough cedar bench. It was twilight; red and purple clouds rippled across the western sky. The mountains to the north and east were already shrouded in darkness, their jutting silhouettes pointing like fingers at yellow-white pinpoints of stars.

The oil spill topic was wrung out, Gilbert found, and guaranteed to lower the mood by leading to discussion of the spill's antecedents, fossil fuels forced from the ground and burned like cigarettes, feeding the terminal cancers of the world. He turned instead to his stock of funny anecdotes about his kids, and stories of fishing trips gone awry. Anne took his cue and got him laughing about the time she tried out for the cheerleading squad and accidentally gave another girl a black eye. Story followed story like silver links in a chain. He went inside, and returned with blankets. It got dark, and they lowered their voices. A dog howled on a neighbouring street, setting others off, like a pack of wolves surrounding them. They fell silent, listening. Gilbert reached over and held Anne's hand.

There was a hot spark, and plenty of dry tinder.

Anne yawned, and confessed the need to sleep. Gilbert helped her to her feet, and drew her closer. They stood facing each other, her head tilted up and his down, tasting each other's breath. She reached up with a finger and traced the broad lines of his lips. He combed his fingers through the silk of her honey-coloured hair. They kissed tenderly, then with pressing passion.

Gilbert pulled away first.

"Let's go for a walk."

They held hands, and barely spoke. Gilbert felt current flowing from her body into his, and his out to hers. The sun had set an hour earlier but a thin line of orange bordered the western horizon, drawing out the day. A light breeze brought salt in from the ocean. He was giddy, lightheaded, like a teenager on a date with the pretty girl from three desks down, one row over. They kissed again. He pressed the centre of her back into him, his breathing shallow, pulse quick.

"Is this okay? I mean, do you want...?"

"I do," she said. "I really do."

They hurried back to his cabin, and tiptoed up the porch steps. Inside, the gentle snores coming from Jonathan's mattress in the corner were like a toddler's, deep and innocent. Gilbert led Anne into his bedroom, where the scenery of his ceiling was invisible in the night. He tugged a sweater off over his head; her legs got caught up in the bunches of her jeans, and she toppled onto the rumpled sheets. He mapped her body, smooth, soft and white, an arctic landscape. She ran her hands along his legs, around his ass, the slight sag of flesh around his middle. She explored his dark nipples, the geography of his chest, with her teeth. When he entered her, she wound her hand in his hair, and pulled his head up and back. He cried out briefly, surprised.

In the morning she was there beside him, her head propped up on her palm, watching him wake up. They kissed, and began again, but the sound of utensils rattling in the kitchen distracted Gilbert. He tried to ignore it, then came the jittery smash of china breaking. He heard water running, and the stove door opening and slamming shut again and again. *Whoops!* There was another crash of crockery splintering, and Gilbert rolled onto his back.

Tentative tap of knuckles on his bedroom door.

"You'd better cover up, he's probably going to -"

The door creaked open. Jonathan pushed his face in, sparse hairs poking from his chin and upper lip, his long hair wound into a knot on the crown of his head.

"Hey man, g'morning. I, like, broke a cup and a plate. Sorry. My bum legs are kind of throwing me off." He craned his neck, working to see past Gilbert's naked torso to Anne's wide-eyed, blushing face. She was holding the twisted sheets at her neckline, draped over the mounds of her breasts. Jonathan's brief veil of confusion fell, and he grinned.

"Oh, hey, hi. Cool. Uh, does this mean I can have the couch now?"

Tlingit

Hungry, I am hungry, and nothing, there is nothing. Not wanting to return to stinking Man Mountain, where there are dangers, bangs of man-claws that reach inside and rip flesh. Man-claw dangers, and things to eat. Bears, other bears, all of us waiting for ice. Slow ice never comes. Ice slow why?

Hungry! Tlingit's mouth pours water, jaws imagine closing on flesh. Follow line of desperate bears to the stinking Man Mountain. Food smells mean food. Think K'ytuk. Do not think K'ytuk, cub who could not swim from ice to shore. Tlingit's cub she could not save.

Belly aches. Ravenous bears have come to the Man Mountain, and here there are men. O danger. Danger and hunger fight each other like wolves inside Tlingit. There is always nothing for eating, and here there is strangeness in the closeness of man-shapes. Man comes close to Tlingit. I charge to make him run away. BOOM! BOOM! *The man-claw bites!*

Hunger fades behind pain. Coming to the Man Mountain was a mistake. Beyond hunger, death was hiding, lurking close to take Tlingit where K'ytuk went before. Now sleep, why sleep? It must be death, falling over Tlingit like night. I fight death, even for this starving, iceless life I fight.

Ah.

CHURCHILL

Ian was beginning to understand why Anne had smacked Jane in the face with his binoculars.

"You can't say it's Tlingit. You didn't have enough data to positively identify the bear." Jane didn't look up from her computer monitor.

"Why don't *you* identify her? She's at the holding facility. I told Frank we would both come as soon as possible. She needs her vitals checked, and I suspect she needs treatment for malnutrition. I want to examine her while she's still unconscious, so I'm going. Right now. Are you coming?"

"The Alert Program has its own veterinarian. My services are not required in this instance."

"But you're a scientist, a biologist! Aren't you even curious? Put your antipathy toward Anne out of your head for a minute, Jane. Forget that this bear is special to her. Think of Tlingit as B127, a particularly at-risk animal we've been following closely for over a year."

He started stuffing a few things in a backpack: callipers, his camera, a couple of Anne's photographs of Tlingit. Jane returned to her computer station and appeared to be engaged with her work, but Ian knew better. He could sense the hot magma bubbling below her surface. If Anne were here, she would be calling Jane out on her indifferent response, but Ian ignored it.

He was throwing the truck into reverse in the parking lot when Jane exited the front doors of the research centre. She walked to his vehicle, opened the passenger door, slid inside, and stared directly ahead. They didn't speak.

Frank Hobbes met them in the foyer of the holding facility.

"Hurry. Stu wants to assess her, and then wake her as soon as possible. She's underweight, so the anaesthetic really walloped her."

The curious medicinal smell of a veterinarian's office permeated the air. The office was cheap, bare bones: linoleum tile floors, fluorescent light fixtures, walls painted a uniform eggshell white. In the surgical room, the bear Ian had tranquilized lay unconscious on a wide stainless steel surface. Money saved on the building's construction had been reallocated to equipment – the table was also a hydraulic lift, like a dentist's chair, allowing for the easy raising and lowering of animals weighing in at hundreds of pounds. There were costly surgical tools as well, monitors and operating room instruments, and a blinding examination light.

Stuart, the program's veterinarian, started speaking as soon as they entered.

"She's used up all of her fat stores. She's two-hundred-ninety-eight pounds, on the light side of the light side. Nothing else is particularly wrong with her, as far as I can tell. She's been in her fair share of scraps I would say. Quite a distinctive scar on her muzzle."

"Her name is Tlingit," said Jane.

Ian raised an eyebrow. Jane ignored him. She spoke to Stuart woodenly, as though she were dictating, or reciting a memorized speech.

"This bear lost a cub in the springtime. The cub drowned. Tlingit exhibited unusual behaviour, including some vocalization of a nature that was hitherto unrecorded. The vocalization gave the impression of expressing grief or loss. It appeared to be a reaction to the loss of her cub. These behaviours were duly recorded, and they are currently the subject of a study being conducted by our intern, Anne McCraig." Jane cleared her throat.

"Thank you, Doctor Minoto," said Ian gently.

Jane's eyes became slightly fluid. "Let's proceed," she said.

Ian hadn't been around tranquilized bears often. When he was, he never had complete confidence the drugs would work. He expected an indignant eye to open, a paw twice the size of his head to swat him, breaking his neck. Tlingit was a female, and small—the smallest adult polar bear he had ever seen—but still, for all that, an impressive creature. He took a deep breath and stepped up beside Stuart, in front of Tlingit's muzzle.

The great black pads on her paws were as wide across as his forearm was long, the better to distribute her weight on the ice. Her claws were thick, greenish-black curved weapons, her shoulders immense masses of muscle. She was perfect, Ian thought, an efficient carnivore, a beautiful killer. Her mandible was one smooth long line. Polar bears successfully hunted beluga whales. The scars on her muzzle were badass, Ian thought. She was a scrapper.

But like all bears, he knew she was also capable of tenderness, affection, and playfulness. He moved closer to her great lolling head and smoothed the fur between her ears. He resisted, then indulged the urge to push his fingers through the deeper, whiter fur around her neck. It was oily, coarse, and surprisingly tough. He marvelled at that hair, not white but transparent and hollow, each strand a tiny air-warming capsule. Her skin was hot underneath his fingers, and black, the better to capture and retain heat. She was perfectly designed for her environment, an evolutionary miracle. For the millionth time, Ian wished he could wind back the hands of time and maintain a realm of cold, ice and snow in the Arctic.

Up close like this, Tlingit didn't seem to be starving. There was so *much* of her. Stuart was busy with the callipers, measuring her belly and shoulder fat. If she was going to survive the lean months, she needed fat, a lot of fat, but Stuart was making *tsk-tsk* noises as he worked.

"I would like five fifteen-cc syringes of her blood," said Jane. She was standing closer to the wall than the bear, tense, immobile. Stuart nodded, finished his measurements and exited the surgery, leaving Ian and Jane alone with Tlingit.

"Touch her," said Ian.

"It isn't necessary."

"Lots of things aren't *necessary.* Bungee jumping, painting a picture, going to the symphony. This is an opportunity for an experience, and you're missing out."

Jane pressed her lips tight together, and her shoulders contracted.

"She's out cold, you know."

"I know that."

As if at gunpoint, Jane edged forward to the bear. She reached out with a small hand and placed it, flat, on Tlingit's topmost foreleg. She hadn't expected it either, Ian saw: the toughness, the raw practicality, the unique arrangement of cells that made up this animal. He watched Jane try, and fail, to resist the same impulse he had felt. She sunk her hand into the dense ruff of fur at Tlingit's neck. She inhaled the bear's earthy, exotic scent.

Stuart clattered into the surgery with the syringes. Jane pulled her hand away from Tlingit and retreated to her clinical position near the wall.

"She's not going to make it without natural food sources, and distance from human populations. She can't thrive in her current location." Stuart plunged a needle into the bear's haunch. The little plastic vial immediately filled with dark red fluid. He replaced the vial with another one. "She's a marginal candidate for relocation, because she's so thin, but I think we should try. We can't even feed her much here, other than IV fluids – it will confuse her. So we need to expedite this thing, and we'll have to take her farther north than Wager Bay. Fifty or a hundred kilometres further north, I think, to find stable ice at this time of year. Frank says we can move her tomorrow. Can you guys come? We could use your expertise."

"She'll sleep until then, though, right?" Ian asked.

Jane's head whipped up.

"What? No, absolutely not! It's dangerous for her to remain anaesthetized. Unfortunately for her, she will have to experience a night of confinement here."

Ian blinked, shocked at Jane's vehemence. Stuart nodded in agreement. Jane met Ian's eyes for the first time in days, and she shook her head at him as if to say, *you idiot.*

"Hey, what do I know? I'm just the plant guy."

KITIMAT

Gilbert called Charlotte in Terrace every day, anxious about the arrival of his next grandchild. In his kitchen, Gilbert held the phone to his right ear and smiled. After Clara died, and after the pipeline was built, he had pretended to be cheerful for Charlotte's sake. Now he was pretending again, but this time dampening evidence of his delight. He hadn't dated another woman since Clara died, and he didn't know how Max and Charlotte would feel about his romance with Anne. Maybe it was too soon, for them.

"How are you, Dad? I'm still not in labour, by the way. Before you ask."

"I'm fine, daughter. Spent another day skimming oil off the river."

"Oh, Dad. I can't believe it, it makes me so mad. What about the Spirit bear, with the oily paws, have you found it?" Charlotte expected her father to be depressed, he could tell. Her sympathy was thick and syrupy.

"Gary flies for an hour every day but still there's no sign. If Moksgm'ol doesn't want to be found, he won't be."

"Do you still have your house guests, the polar bear lady and the grizzly boy, or whatever?"

Gilbert paused. He could Anne and Jonathan laughing outside in the garden, his strange little oil spill family, harvesting squash and kale. He was careful to keep his voice even, noncommittal.

"Yeah, they're still here. Jonathan's much better, his scratches are healing. He can help with the spill soon. In the meantime, he cooks and cleans. Pretty good guest."

The pleasure he felt being with Anne was so intense, Gilbert imagined it spoke loudly into the silence on the phone, and he waited for Charlotte to pick up on it. He and Anne were cautious in public. In the cabin, around Jonathan, they felt free, and kissed and hugged. But downtown and at the cleanup sites, Anne was self-conscious, mostly because Gilbert's friends were there, and they had all known Clara. Anne said she didn't want to be *that* woman, the next woman, the one who wasn't Clara, who wouldn't be good enough, or native enough, for Gilbert.

"What about Max, have you heard from him?"

"Things are busy for him at the tire shop. I guess that's why I haven't seen him, much."

Max had despised his father's ardent activism against the pipeline. His son had been a proponent of the thing, to Gilbert's dismay. But it wasn't that surprising. Max's friends were the sons and daughters of loggers, of employees of Kitimat's aluminum smelter, and of commercial fishers. They were trophy hunters and resource-extractors and they wanted big, new trucks and four-bedroom houses. When Clara was alive, she had possessed the power to temper Max's bouts of sullen resentment over what their son saw as the Crow family's poverty. When his mother died, it seemed that Max's interest in his ancestors and traditional way of life died with her.

"You're living in the past, Dad. Money makes the world go round, and natural resources make money. There's no use sticking your head in the sand. You can't turn back the clock and stop driving. You can't paddle everywhere in a canoe, and heat your house with wood."

"I heat my house with wood."

"Your tiny cabin, you mean. Nobody lives the way you do anymore."

"*I* live the way I do."

"Yeah, well, most people don't. And don't pretend you're different - you've got your truck, you drive around, everybody needs fuel. The pipeline means more jobs in Kitimat, and more people moving here. Everyone's going to benefit, including you. If you want to go back to living in a longhouse and hunting and fishing, dig in. But don't hang around Kitimat whining about the pipeline. The rest of us need the work."

Nothing could change Max's mind, not the scant number of permanent jobs the pipeline promised, not the potential loss of jobs in recreation and adventure tourism if the unthinkable – a spill – happened. Gilbert and his son had argued, lightly and theoretically at first, then with steadily growing vehemence and venom. The last time they went fishing together had led to their worst fight, and they hadn't been fishing together since. On that morning the mist hung over the river, eagles called and dove, and a black bear ambled along the north shore. Gilbert swept his arm across the panorama.

"This is what you and your buddies take for granted. It won't be here for you, if there's a spill. Not like this, never the same."

"If! You guys are a bunch of Chicken Littles, running around saying that the sky is falling. The sky isn't going to fall. *Old* pipelines fail. This one will be brand new."

Max had dropped his fishing rod and walked away.

And then the sky fell. It wasn't like Gilbert to call his son and say he told him so. But every day of the cleanup he nursed a hope, an expectation almost, that he would glance up to see Max walking toward him on the oily beach, rolling up his shirtsleeves to lend a hand. When he told Charlotte things were busy at the tire shop, Gilbert was making excuses for Max.

But then, Max had never wanted to work more than he had to. It was because of laziness, Gilbert guessed, that selling the Creator's gifts appealed to his son. Harvest and profit, easy money.

Gilbert said goodbye to Charlotte, still thinking about Max.

He remembered a day, many years ago, when he had asked Max to help stack firewood. Thick, menacing clouds had been sweeping inland that day, racing toward the mountains, bearing down on Kitimat. Gilbert had split a pyramid of wood as tall as himself, and to keep it dry it had to be stacked and tarped. Clara and Charlotte had pitched in, the first fat raindrops pinging off the metal cabin roof. Max had been eight or nine years old, sitting in the gravelly sand of the driveway, playing with his little metal cars.

"Max. Rain is coming. Help us put this wood away."

"No."

Frustration simmering, Gilbert had mastered his feelings and squelched the desire to yell at his son.

"Would you like to hear a story?"

"Sure."

Moksgm'ol Teaches a Lesson

It was autumn, and time to prepare for winter. There was meat and fish to smoke and preserve. There were berries to harvest, clothes to make and repair, and houses to patch and finish. All the people of a certain village were working together, singing songs and telling stories. All except Taaku, who was hiding. Taaku was sitting on a rock by the estuary, throwing stones into the water. He was supposed to be collecting firewood, but it seemed like too much work, and he didn't want to.

Taaku saw a seal swimming in the water, rolling casually and lazily from its smooth silver back to its speckled front. The seal's glossy fur shimmered where the sun struck its coat, its whiskers twitched, and it was smiling. *Look at Seal,* Taaku thought, *relaxing, doing as he pleases. No one is asking Seal to gather wood, or gut fish, or clean hides to make winter cloaks! I wish I could be Seal.*

Then Taaku said the words he was thinking out loud.

"I wish *I* could be Seal. I wish *I* could be Seal."

Moksgm'ol, the Spirit bear, was nearby, listening to Taaku. The Spirit bear had special powers given to him by the Great Bear, and he decided to use them now. Moksgm'ol turned the young man into a seal.

At first, Taaku was delighted. He flexed his new lithe body in the water, diving down farther and longer than he had ever dared to dive as a human. He rolled on the surface, loving the coolness of the water and the freedom of his new water home. He grew bold, and began to splash his tail-fin at the surface of the water. He let out happy barks, speaking to his friends on the shore.

"Look at me! I have no chores! I can play in the water all day!" Taaku splashed and barked, showing off to the hard-working people of his village.

But Taaku caught the interest of a hungry orca whale. He saw the big black dorsal fin slicing through the water toward him, and he began to swim away as quickly as he could, undulating his seal body. It was no use. The orca whale was gaining on him. He swam toward shore, hoping to enter water that was too shallow for the black-and-white whale. The orca was almost close enough to bite Taaku in half when the seal-boy saw an eagle, soaring high above him. Fervently he barked a plea.

"I wish I were Eagle! I wish I were Eagle!"

Moksgm'ol, still watching from his place in the forest, granted the boy's next wish. In a flash, Taaku ceased to be a seal and was instead an eagle, soaring high above the treetops, looking down on the black back of a confused and disappointed whale.

"Ha ha!" screamed the young eagle-man. "No one can touch me now, for I have no predators. I fly, free and unfettered, far above my village! Look at them all, slaving away down there, while I have the wind under my feathers, and not a care in the world!"

Taaku soared above the trees for a day and a half. The people of his village wondered and worried about his absence, and Taaku laughed his shrill screaming laugh at them from the sky. But it wasn't long before he got lonely. He tried to talk to other eagles, but they ignored him completely, or chased him away. The loneliness became a painful ache. Below him, he saw a herd of black-tailed deer standing in a clearing and feeding together. His heart longed for camaraderie, and he screeched another request.

"I wish I were Deer! I wish I were Deer!"

And then he was a deer, running over the fields and through the forests, surrounded by other deer. He hooked his small antlers with those of other young bucks, and played with them. At night he slept with the herd, and he was warm, and heartened by the companionship. He grew smug as he remembered all the work the people of his village had to do, while Taaku the young deer-man spent his days eating and wandering idly through the forest.

Winter arrived with its cold and snow. One day, Taaku wandered too far from the herd, and found himself face to face with a hungry black bear. The bear stood on its hind legs, snarling its displeasure. Taaku tried to run away, but the hungry bear was at his hooves, so close that the bear's hot breath warmed his floppy tail. In a panic, without thinking, he wished:

"Make me Bear! I want to be Bear!"

Immediately Taaku became a black bear, and turned to face his pursuer. Scared and amazed, the attacking bear ran away into the forest. Taaku felt pangs of hunger in his big bear-belly. He followed his nose toward the good smells of smoked meat and fish coming from the village nearby.

When he got close, Taaku realized that it was his own village. He emerged from a thicket and abruptly came upon a beautiful young woman. He recognized her; she was the loveliest young woman in his village. She was carrying a basket, collecting firewood. Taaku was torn by his twin desires. He wanted to eat the young woman and assuage his hunger, and he also wanted to kiss her.

The young woman saw Taaku's bear-form, and she dropped her basket. She didn't run from him, but lifted her chin and faced him with impunity, fierce and unafraid. His human heart was won by her courage, and he once again implored the air around him:

"I wish I were a Man once more. I wish I were a Man!"

Moksgm'ol took pity on Taaku, and gave him back his human form. The young woman was surprised. She gasped and she blushed, confronted by this tall, strong young man with a handsome countenance. She didn't recognize Taaku.

"Why are you alone?" Taaku asked her. "It's almost winter, and the bears are hungry. It's dangerous to wander alone."

"My village desperately needs firewood. We had too much work this harvest season, and not enough people to do it. Our elders and babies are cold. The young and strong must help the old and weak, naturally."

Then Taaku finally saw the error of his ways, and understood how lazy he had been, and how his family suffered because of his indolence. He returned to his village with the young woman. Every day he collected wood and hunted. He was rewarded for his efforts with the respect of his village, and the love of the beautiful young woman.

"What did you think about that story?"

"Bad," Max had answered, kicking at the gravel in the driveway. "You're just trying to make me do stuff I don't want to do. And I don't like girls. They're yucky."

* * *

Gilbert was on the front porch, talking to his daughter on the phone. Jonathan was going for a walk, limping down to the river by himself. Anne made herself a cup of instant coffee, opened her laptop, and cleared a space at the kitchen table. Lumpy pillows were tied to the seats of the old wooden kitchen chairs. The pillows were homemade, fashioned from an ugly brown fabric with pictures of purple grapes. She adjusted a pillow underneath her bum, which today felt perfect. Today Anne was inside her skin, taking up her space in the world, content with how she fit into the air around her. The way the underside of her breasts grazed the edge of the table, the spread of her ass on the pillow, the smooth circumference of her forearms resting beside the keyboard – everything about Anne's body was ideal.

And nothing had changed. Nothing external had changed. A remarkable man found her interesting, beautiful, and desirable, and that was enough. Anne wanted to beat herself up for needing those outside eyes to find her attractive. Why couldn't she love her body all by herself, without help? The question pricked at her, but she was too content to let it niggle.

She had come to Gilbert naked, without clothes and without pretense. She had told him her body was a foreign thing, a meat puppet, a skin she wriggled in uncomfortably, and the telling took away the power of the illusion. Her confession was the magic trick that revealed the flawless body underneath her brutal judgement of herself. Recklessly, she was falling in love with Gilbert. Anne was blonde and round, slow in the winter, and she loved to eat, sleep and play. She was his human Spirit bear, and she thought she felt him falling in love with her, too.

She squirted a dollop of honey into her tea and stirred, then licked the spoon, relishing the sweetness. On the front porch, Gilbert laughed.

Her heart leapt as if a creature the size of a chipmunk had twitched in her chest, and her head tingled with dizzy infatuation. *Get a hold of yourself.* She flipped open the laptop, opened her mail program, and typed.

Dear Ian,

I hope you're okay, alone out there with Jane. How are 'our' bears? I got the group email with the weekly numbers, but I don't have time to go over the data. I'm working ten hour days.

You're probably wondering how bad the spill is, and what the cleanup looks like. It's worse than the media is reporting. It's the ecologically worst-case scenario, a marine spill. Lots of oil has gotten past booms on the Kitimat River, so the oil is in the food chain. The cleanup is – well – take a jar of white sugar to a sandy, breezy beach. Pour the sugar onto the sand, and spread it out. Now pick up all of the sugar, grain by grain. That's the challenge, but that's not why I'm writing.

There's a bear in trouble, and I need your help. I'm staying with a man, Gilbert Crow. He watches the Spirit bear population around Kitimat, it's his thing. On the day of the spill, a Spirit bear was seen running through the spill area, its paws black with oil. Gilbert says he knows this bear, and he's determined to find it, and help it. Oil or no oil, the bear needs to be relocated. It has made downtown Kitimat its home, and that can't be.

There's no one who can do a relocation here. I can hire a helicopter pilot, check the bear's vitals, and outfit it with a transceiver so we can monitor its progress afterward. You're the best marksman I know Ian. I need you to come anaesthetize this bear. Actually, a hemobiographical analysis would tell us if the bear has been affected by oil toxins, but I know Jane won't come.

Let me know ASAP ok?

Xo Anne

Kitimat

It was midmorning in the Kitimat cabin. Gilbert and Anne, the coolest middle aged people on the planet in Jonathan's opinion, had left hours ago for another day of cleaning up oil. Every day when they get home, they tell Jonathan about the work he's missing. So far they have washed beaches, transported stricken birds, shovelled up oily wood chips in the forest, and acted as crew members on a boat siphoning oil from the Kitimat River. Jonathan longed to be out there with them, being the eco-warrior of his imagination. But in spite of antibiotics and gobs of topical cream, the lacerations on his thigh were infected, a painful setback to his recovery.

He was tired of cooking, which had been fun at first, trying to use as much of Gilbert's vegetable garden as he could at each meal. His repertoire was limited; he alternated between spaghetti and salad, and salmon and salad. Gilbert and Anne didn't complain. They were in love, Jonathan saw. It was his first close-up, real-life experience watching two people in love. His parents loved each other in a durable marriage, peck-on-the-cheek way. Gilbert and Anne were like cinematic lovers, lost in each other's eyes, impulsively hair-tousling and holding hands. They managed to conduct their romance without making him feel like a third wheel. Anne liked flexing her untested maternal muscles on him, gently instructing him about the best way to poach an egg, or sweep the floor.

And Gilbert had fatherly advice for him. Some evenings, they walked down to the river, following the path Gilbert used to take with his children, and like a small child, Jonathan needed help climbing over logs and negotiating slippery sections. Autumn was beginning to hint at winter, the sky when it was visible was pale, barely blue, fending off thick charcoal clouds scudding in from the ocean.

One afternoon, Gilbert had knelt down beside a humble plant with a thorny stem and broad, flat leaves. "This plant is used by my people to treat skin conditions. You crush the leaves, and mix them with hot water to create a paste. It only grows in older forests. Find it again tomorrow, and make the paste, and treat your leg." But Jonathan hadn't done this.

On the stony riverbank they had perched on a large, flat rock.

"Sit here and watch the animals come and go. Sit quietly, and you will see some of our Haisla clan animals, Eagle and Raven, Beaver and Crow.

"White people don't have that kind of relationship with animals. I've got a story for you." Jonathan had told Gilbert the story of his great-grandfather, Lothar, and the Kolner Zoo, and the firebombing of Cologne.

"Did all of the animals die?"

"I guess so. I mean, they must have."

"That is a terrible story, Jonathan. Your ancestor's spirit was very sick. There was a disease of the spirit then I think, a contagious disease, and many people were infected with it. Destroying the earth to make money is a contagious disease of the spirit, and it has spread all over the planet. There are people who spread the disease on purpose, like some European settlers did, giving smallpox-infected blankets. But there are many others who inadvertently catch the disease from their parents and their friends.

"This oil spill is a symptom of the bigger disease. Humans talk about the economy as though it's something as real as this river that is running to the sea in front of us. But the economy could collapse—all of the money, real and imagined, could disappear tomorrow—and this river will keep running to the sea. Whether or not it runs clean and full of fish that we can eat and water that we can drink depends on how sick we are with the spiritual disease."

Jonathan thought a lot about what Gilbert said that day. He searched the internet, still wondering what had happened to the zoo animals in Cologne during and after the firebombing. His searches came up with nothing about the animals, until on a whim he typed *Happy the panda.*

The panda had survived! Happy was bought by a zoo in Saint Louis, Missouri, shortly after Cologne was bombed. The panda lived another few years in the Saint Louis Zoo, and died there in 1946. For some reason this news cheered Jonathan. Maybe great granddaddy Lothar wasn't such a bad guy, after all. Maybe he had been out there with buckets or a hose, rescuing the captive animals from being burned alive.

Clicking through panda hits, Jonathan found live streaming video of a mother panda cuddling her newborn at the San Diego Zoo. The sprawling mother panda held a tiny, perfect replica of herself, tucked sweetly in her arms. He got sleepy watching them cuddle, and rested his head in his arms on the table. He woke up suddenly half an hour later with reddish squares on his left cheek, the imprint of the keyboard. He was alarmed to discover he had drooled extensively. Clear fluid pooled between the 7, 8 and 9, and trickled down to N, M, and the space bar. He scrambled awkwardly to wipe the keyboard dry with his sleeve, creating havoc on the monitor. *Aw, man!* He spent the rest of the morning staring at the monitor and clicking the mouse, trying to return Gilbert's desktop to the way it was before he had touched it.

Churchill

Ian and Jane left the polar bear holding facility before Stuart revived Tlingit. Citing a backlog of work, Jane requested they head back to the research centre. Ian suspected that, like him, she didn't want to watch Tlingit come to, didn't want to see the polar bear sow's fear and confusion when she woke to her stark human surroundings. Tlingit would spend just one night in a concrete cell, and never know how fortunate she was. Many of the captured bears spent weeks pacing a cramped space behind steel bars and stained plexiglass, waiting for Hudson Bay to freeze over entirely so they could be released onto the ice. Ian and Jane would meet Stuart and two other members of a bear transport team, including the helicopter pilot, at the holding facility at seven the next morning.

Staring blankly through the truck's windshield, Jane was a dam about to break. Ian sensed water seeping through stress fractures in the thick concrete of her retaining wall. She was showing a vulnerability that had been missing since he met her, and Ian was determined to take advantage of this softening, and draw her out. They drove along the bleak washed-out highway silently until he volunteered to make dinner. With a curt bob of her head, Jane accepted.

The menu, Ian guessed, was an essential part of breaking through Dr. Minoto's defences. He cooked her favourite foods: a light salad with apples and pine nuts, white rice fluffed with butter and salt, herbed and fried whitefish filets, a bottle of crisp white wine. Whistling and bustling in the kitchen, Ian surprised himself by dropping only a single rice-laden fork. Ordinarily his culinary excursions were messy affairs. He missed Anne laughing at him as he bumbled around looking for the cheese grater, or left the tap running to run and save a sauce from burning.

Jane joined him at six o'clock precisely, the collar of her shirt buttoned up to the hollow in her throat, her hands folded in perfect symmetry on the table in front of her.

"This is an excellent dinner, thank you Ian."

"My pleasure. More wine?"

"Perhaps a splash."

"I appreciated your professionalism today," he said as he poured, not meeting her eyes.

She lifted her eyebrows in mild surprise.

"It was a difficult day."

"I agree, but why? Why was it so hard for you, I mean?" Ian stared into his wine glass, swirled the pale liquid, watched it wash up the glass, cling, and then recede. He could feel words bubbling up close to Jane's quiet surface. She looked out the window across from her, where twilight was already deepening to darkness. He heard an imaginary clock ticking, a weighted second hand nudging time forward. From where he sat, Ian could see Jane's reflection in the window glass. She opened her mouth, closed it, then spoke at last.

"In 1941, my grandfather was placed in an internment camp in Greenwood, B.C. You know about them, right?"

Ian nodded. He didn't risk interrupting her flow.

"Before Greenwood, he was a peaceful man, a commercial fisherman in Steveston, south of Vancouver. He lived simply, he was content to fish and play cards. My grandmother sold his catch in the market. She was taken to the camp too, and so was their oldest son, Akira. He was only five. My father, Tomo, was born in the internment camp." Jane paused, and closed her eyes.

"The camp changed my grandfather. He became angry and bitter. He taught his children to trust no one, and he was strict to the point of being abusive. My uncle remembers cold showers every morning, and beatings with a leather strap for acting goofy with white kids. Tomo and Akira were allowed only the bare minimum of possessions, and no toys. My grandfather was paranoid after the camp. He imagined strangers were actually spies for the Canadian government, keeping tabs on the Japanese population.

"My father swore he wouldn't be like my grandfather. He allowed us, my sister and brother and me, all the toys and clothes we desired and could afford. But there was one thing he refused to consider, even though we kids wanted it very badly. It was a frivolous thing, not a necessity. We desperately wanted a pet—a puppy."

Jane swallowed. She put her wine glass down and twined her fingers together, squeezing, her knuckles turning white.

"My father forbade it, and my mother honoured him in all things, and wouldn't hear our pleas. Once, we were on the boardwalk in Steveston, and my sister saw an adorable cocker spaniel, and asked my father again if we could get a puppy. When we got home he slapped her, hard, across her face, but still I didn't understand the depth of my father's feelings on this issue. Later on, after we were grown up, my mother explained that for my father, caring for a non-human living creature was an ostentatious waste of resources, and a path to heartbreak. My grandparents had owned two dogs, you see, dogs that they loved very much. Their dogs were taken forcibly from them when they were imprisoned at the internment camp. They never saw those dogs again."

There was more to the story, Ian could tell. He held his breath, scraping his fork across his plate, gathering the last flakes of fish and grains of rice. He could hear Jane's breathing, short and forced, as if she had been running.

"One afternoon a friends' mother showed up in the elementary school parking lot with a cardboard box. Inside was a litter of eight or nine puppies. I don't know what breed they were – cute, longhaired, black-and-white puppies. They were free, my friend's mother said, anybody could take one. They were adorable, and I thought if I brought one home, my father would fall in love with it, and see how much joy it brought his children. I thought he and my mother would give in, and let us keep it."

"You were wrong," Ian whispered.

"I was wrong. My father was working a nine-to-five day job. We got home from school before him, and we managed to hide Scooter—I named him—in the backyard for two whole days before my parents discovered he was there. I don't know how my mother didn't figure it out earlier. Scooter must have slept all day while we were at school. He was tied up under the porch.

"On the third day, we ran home from school, giddy and excited to play with our puppy. When we got home, my father's car was parked in front of the house. For a brief second, I had the crazy hope he would tell us we could keep Scooter. Then I saw my mother's face in the window. She was crying, something she never did. The three of us kids ran around behind the house. My father was standing with a shovel in his hand next to a fresh pile of dirt. *I told you*, he said, *no pets.*"

Jane was crying, her body jolting rhythmically with suppressed sobs. There was nothing Ian could say. He reached out for her hands, but she snatched them off the table and turned her head from him.

"Jane."

"Would you leave me alone, please?"

"No. Being alone isn't going to make it easier."

Jane stamped a foot in frustration. She dragged the backs of her hands across her eyes. Her shoulders bounced up and down. Ian stood, pushing back his chair so hard it toppled to the floor. He snatched a box of tissues from the top of the refrigerator and dropped it on the table in front of Jane.

"What's amazing is, your father didn't quell your passion for animals. You still pursued a career in biology."

Jane sniffed. She glared at Ian, and sneered.

"My father is ashamed of me. He wanted me to be a medical doctor. In his estimation, I am a failure."

Ian picked up his chair and folded himself into it.

"Then your father is a fool. You're hugely successful in the scientific field of your choice. You're brilliant, Jane. You must know how many applicants competed for these Churchill positions. You edged out—by an impressive margin, I understand—hundreds of your peers. And I've been watching you work. Everything you do is accurate and thorough. You're such an asset to this team."

Jane pulled her head into her neck, as if compliments crushed her from the top down.

"I really want you to come to Kitimat with me."

"What?"

"There's a kermode bear. Its paws are contaminated with oil, and it urgently needs relocation. There are probably more at-risk bears in the contamination zone. I know you've been following the news. This spill is a national environmental emergency. I spoke to the Arctic Research Institute and they are in agreement, we can suspend our research here in Manitoba to help out in British Columbia. I pulled some strings and got us a couple of rooms at the Pacific Motor Inn in Kitimat. You're a national expert in ursine risk assessment. We wouldn't have to stay long, we could complete our report back here, in Churchill."

Ian piled up an inelegant stack of dishes, and balanced it on his forearms. He made it to the sink without dropping anything. In the window, he watched Jane take a slow sip of wine. She wasn't saying no, which meant that against the odds, she was considering the proposition.

Tlingit

Disaster – caught! Press of man-place, dream-yet-not-a-dream. Pungent man-stink in my fur. The light of man comes from a small round ball. Blank, empty, nothing inside nothing.

Numb, I am numb everywhere, like the pads of my feet on the coldest day. Numbness is inside my head, and tingling, and pain. Pressing into flat rocks, sniffing corners, but no escape. It is disaster, Tlingit is caught. Nothing to eat, no little K'ytuk. Hunger, and numbness.

Slowly, walk slowly, few steps and turn, few steps and turn. Push face between hard thin lines. Tlingit's body will not squeeze between the lines. I have no strength. From bad-no-sea-ice, to worse-no-K'ytuk, to disaster.

Man! A man stands close, so close I could bite him, taste his blood, and eat his flesh, if not for the hard lines. Into my numb ears the man makes man-noises. Terror, bad dream, disaster!

From the Man Mountain I have arrived at nowhere. This is death, perhaps. No ice, no water, no sky, no snow. Now there is no world of the bear. I lift a paw and swat the hard lines, and the man disappears.

No world of the bear.

Latitude 60 Degrees North

Ian watched Jane, who had the window seat in the back of the helicopter. She was craning her neck to keep the shape of Tlingit, dangling in a net below and behind them, in sight. He could picture what Jane saw: a white ball of fur caught in a net, pressed into an unnatural shape, all her bearish majesty collapsed into an undignified, human-managed contraption. A flying bear, swinging like a pom-pom on a strand of white wool, buffeted by wind and velocity.

It was heartrending somehow, more so because the bear was Tlingit, the bear Anne loved, the mother bear they had heard crying over her drowned cub. Tlingit, whose images surrounded them in the hallways of the research station. She was equipped with two transceivers now, one in her skin, and another in her gum line. They would be able to track her, monitor her progress, assure themselves by her movements that she was alive, and hopefully thriving in her new colder and more remote hunting grounds.

Tlingit was lightly sedated. Her eyes were smeared with Vaseline to protect them from ice and wind. Stuart had assured them before take-off that she would be aware of her surroundings, but nonplussed by them, like a dental patient dosed with Ativan. Other than being moderately to severely malnourished, the bear's condition was good. She fell within the acceptable parameters of relocation risk-benefit analysis – with luck, she would adapt to her new home, and thrive.

Jane was different today, lighter. She had smiled at him at breakfast, and asked how he had slept. A spring inside her had unwound. He knew they would never speak of her father and the puppy again. Jane's story was like a poison gas, released to float away and disperse harmlessly in the stratosphere. *Anne won't recognize her,* Ian thought.

They flew on, further and further north, and with every kilometre of latitude they gained, the ice below them thickened, until the margin between shore and bay became indistinct. The pilot lowered the helicopter over a flat, open area, and Frank executed a hover exit. Crouching he unhooked the net from the tether attaching it to the aircraft. The pilot flew fifty meters away and landed. Ian, Jane and Stuart rushed to meet Frank and Tlingit on the ice.

Thin needles of freezing rain were falling, stinging exposed skin. They opened the net, each of them taking a corner. Tlingit's eyes were open but unfocused, balefully flicking from human to human. Ian thought she seemed aware of her predicament.

"She's scared."

"I doubt it," said Stuart. "She won't remember any of this. Now come on, we have to roll her off the net."

All of them pushed and heaved at the bulk of her. Her great limbs flopped, useless. Stuart held and controlled her head, stabilizing her neck. They rolled her over once, again, and then she was on her side in the snow, free of the net. Stuart pulled a green paint pen from his pocket and drew a large, distinct dot on Tlingit's head. The people of Nunavut would know by this dot that this bear had an anaesthetic drug in her system.

Ian stepped back from the bear and the net. He turned in a slow circle, trying and failing to pull a distinguishing feature out of the ice-smeared landscape. He wouldn't last five minutes out here. Which way was Hudson Bay? Where might there be shelter for the night? The wind was hostile, every horizon was a white vista of endless mystery. But the polar bear, once the taint of drugs wore off, would know where she was, and what to do. How infinitely more suited she was to this place. What good was his human intelligence out here, Ian wondered, when he couldn't meet the fundamental requirements of life? Here in this realm, this frozen enigma, Tlingit was the superior beast.

"Ian, come on, help us out here," Stuart called. They were rubbing handfuls of snow into Tlingit's fur. "This will remove some of our human scent from her fur, and make her more comfortable when she comes out of it."

Ian joined them. Jane was rubbing snow into the bear's thick fur, not bothering to hide the pleasure she was getting from the feel of Tlingit's voluptuous coat. Her thick snow-glasses were fogging up with exertion. She worked snow up the bear's foreleg, into the neck ruff, then halted before the great head, and left her hands immersed in fur. Ian saw Jane wordlessly meet Tlingit, and appreciate the bear, and maybe even dare to love an animal again. His eyes stung, and he turned his head from the intimate moment.

At last they all withdrew, and stood halfway between the bear and the helicopter. They huddled together against the ice needles, whipping them now from the east, now from the southwest. Ian repressed an urge to put a fraternal arm around Jane. *Too much, too soon.* It wasn't long before Tlingit lifted her head and swayed it from side to side, sniffing. She stretched, and then rolled from one side to the other. At last, she stood, then pushed herself back onto her haunches. She swung her head and glared at them, *I know you're there.* Stuart clapped his leather and seal-fur mittens together.

"That's our cue. Back in the bird, everybody."

"I'd prefer to observe her another five minutes."

Jane's mouth was a hard little line, but Stuart shook his head.

"May I remind you how healthy her appetite is at present? We are the nearest source of sashimi. If we wait until she's fully awake, it will probably be the last thing we ever do."

The force of the helicopter's rotors pushed fine snow up into a cloud. Without the green dot on her head, Tlingit would have been hard to spot. The pilot hovered, and the polar bear watched them, then spun around and began loping away from the world of man. Tlingit was alone, and she was free.

Convergence

On the twelfth day of cleanup, Anne and Gilbert got home and found Jonathan more dishevelled than usual. He was wearing an apron smeared with food. There were bits of something orange in his hair, Anne noticed, and his chin had a black smudge in the centre. He called to them from the porch as they stepped out of the truck.

"I hope there's a pizza joint in this town. There's nothing edible for us here. The wood stove is crazy, man. It burns everything. And you're out of dish soap."

Closer up, Anne saw Jonathan's face was sweaty with exertion, and his eyes were rimmed with red. She turned back to Gilbert, who was still sitting behind the wheel in his truck.

He's not okay, Anne mouthed.

"There are *three* pizza joints in this town," Gilbert called through the truck's open window. "Lose the apron, Jonathan. Let's go for a drive."

Jonathan pulled the apron over his head and dropped it where he stood. He hopped down the porch steps using the railing and limped furiously past Anne, shaking his head and muttering.

"Sorry about the mess."

Inside the cabin, a layer of smoke hung around the ceiling. A stack of blackened pots balanced on a cutting board strewn with detritus. Anne smelled the oil on her clothes and in her hair while she scraped eggshells, wilted lettuce, and an ancient, shrivelled mushroom into a steel compost canister. She scraped a frying pan surface with steel wool.

She had lost heart that afternoon, after catching sight of a pail full of oily fish, and she had fled the spill site. Gilbert had found her walking to the cabin. He had pulled the truck to the side of the road and walked to meet her, stopping when they faced each other.

"I can't do it anymore. There's too much damage. I want to turn back the clock to before the spill, before internal combustion engines, before coal and steam and electricity."

"The earth is strong, stronger than us. Believe it, Anne. She wants to breathe and heal. This moment is imperfect, but it's all we have."

Gilbert had wrapped her in his arms, and she had leaned her head on his shoulder. Scrubbing the frying pan, Anne felt a knot in her stomach. Today was all they had, and she had to go back to Churchill and finish her internship. In her mind's eye the research centre was a bleak prison, with Jane guarding the doors and maintaining order. Her cell phone rang, and she dropped the pan into soapy water, dried her hands, and answered. It was Ian.

"Hey, we're at the airport. Any chance you can come pick us up, and take us to our motel?"

"Ian! You never said you were coming, for sure! And who is 'we'?"

"Wanted to surprise you, and you'll see when you get here."

"I can't come, I don't have a car... Have you walked outside? Look for the tallest, widest guy you can see, with a huge nose and glasses. His name is Little Ted, and the beater beside him is his cab. I'll text you his phone number, in case he isn't there, and he'll come get you eventually. Where are you staying?"

"The Pacific Motor Inn. I'm walking outside the airport. Oh, okay. That guy is here. I'm waving at him, and he's waving back. Thanks, Anne. When will we see you?"

"Gilbert and I will come to your motel this evening. Text me your room number once you've checked in. And who is 'we'?"

"Nice try, Anne. See you soon."

An idea struck Anne, and without thinking, she acted on it.

"Hey, tell Little Ted that you and I are engaged, and you're here to win me back from the man who has stolen my heart."

"Having a little fun, are we? I don't know, Anne, are you sure? This guy looks like he might have a heart condition."

"Nah, he'll be okay. Just do it."

Anne and Gilbert drove to the Pacific Motor Inn at twilight. Jonathan wanted to come too, but he was full of painkillers and pizza, and had fallen asleep before they left, stretched out on the beige couch, snoring robustly.

The motel announced itself with a red neon sign on a rusty iron post. It was a low-slung, dilapidated building slumped behind a neglected parking lot, where weeds grew out of cracks and potholes in the asphalt. Gilbert parked in front of a mottled brown door with the number fourteen inexpertly painted on it in white. Little Ted's taxi was parked in front of room number twelve. Gilbert sighed.

"I wish I had space at my cabin for your friends. This place is more rundown than I remembered."

The door to number fourteen swung open. Gilbert and Anne got out of the truck as Little Ted emerged from the motel room.

"Business is good, Ted," Gilbert deadpanned.

"Can't complain," Little Ted pushed his glasses up his nose.

From the shadows behind the cabbie's bulk, a slight person slid out into the dim light outside the motel. It was Jane, and she thoroughly confused Anne by smiling. Ducking to avoid smacking his head on the low doorframe, Ian loped out last, opening his arms toward Anne.

"Here I am, honey! Together at last."

"I swear I didn't know, Gil, when I brought her to your place," said Little Ted.

Gilbert's face had turned to stone, the same petrified look he had worn when Anne first saw him on television, the first day of the oil spill. Regret washed over Anne. She wondered what it was in her nature that made her sabotage her own happiness in spectacular, thoughtless ways. Unable to speak to Gilbert and admit her stupid joke, Anne lashed out at Jane.

"What is *she* doing here?" Anne asked Ian.

The tentative happiness in Jane's expression wobbled precariously.

"You didn't know what?" Gilbert asked Little Ted.

"That she was engaged. I had no idea. I wouldn't have done that to you." Little Ted pointed a fat, accusing finger at Anne.

Anne opened her mouth, and no sound came out. She met Gilbert's eyes and shook her head side to side, her guts convulsing.

They stood in an awkward oval in the parking lot. A chorus of frogs croaked somewhere nearby. A raven flew overhead, low enough that its wing-beats were audible, pushing evenly into the night air. Gilbert spoke slowly.

"I believe... that the joke is on you, Ted."

Ian grinned.

"Anne and I haven't known each other for very long, but I know her well enough. This is someone's idea of a bad joke." said Gilbert. "You must be Ian. Good to meet you." They shook hands.

Jane took off, striding briskly into the darkness.

"She came out here for you, Anne," said Ian.

"Jane, wait!"

Anne followed Jane into the night.

Gilbert's cell phone rang. He held up a finger, smiled ruefully at Ian and Little Ted, and wandered away as he answered the call. He stopped and leaned on a slanted, rusty metal staircase leading up to the motel lobby.

Little Ted and Ian considered each other in silence.

"Sorry," said Ian at last.

"It's okay, I had it coming," Little Ted removed his glasses, squinted, and pinched the bridge of his bulbous nose. "Mom keeps telling me to keep this big ugly thing out of other people's business."

"No hard feelings, then?"

"None at all."

A reverberating *clang, clang clang!* resonated in the parking lot. Gilbert was knocking his head repeatedly on the rickety banister of the motel staircase, punctuating a rhetorical question.

"Why"—*clang*—"does everything"—*clang*— "happen" —*clang*—"at once?"

He left the staircase and walked stiffly back to the rectangle of light cast by the open door of room fourteen, where Ian and Ted were watching him expectantly. Gilbert paused, took a deep breath, and spoke on the exhale.

"My daughter is in labour, and Moksgm'ol is here, in town. It's going to be a long night."

"And an auspicious one," said Little Ted, indicating the northern sky. Long, erratic green and purple lines had materialized above them, leaping, swaying and undulating, a contemporary dance of heavenly scarves, sprinkled with stars like silver sequins. The men cocked their heads back and watched the performance.

Around the corner on a quiet residential street, Jane had heard Anne calling her name, pleading with her to *wait, please, I want to talk to you, hear me out!* Jane turned, and she saw the northern lights spreading across the sky. Anne followed Jane's gaze and gasped, puffing from exertion, her hands on her hips. Anne thought she could hear a hum and crackle from the northern lights.

"Jane, I was rude back there. I'm so surprised you're here, I -"

Without turning her eyes from the celestial show, Jane interrupted Anne.

"I have been rude to you on any number of occasions. We are very different. The way I grew up, your kind of sentimentality – it was disallowed. It is dangerous to me, the way you wear your heart on your sleeve. It's not your fault. I know how you see me, tight and bound and unfeeling. To me you are like an open wound, bleeding out, where I am bandaged."

"Okay. I'm a bleeding wound, that's fair. You're probably right about that. And you are bandaged up so tight, your circulation is cut off."

They watched the purple and green waves bend and flow, throwing off fingers of light in unpredictable patterns, a disordered, organic dance. Anne cleared her throat.

"Sorry, that was mean. Maybe I'm threatened by the way you control everything. I like things messy, I need a little chaos around me to work."

"We are different, as I said. Our natures are black and white, almost. Perhaps not incompatible, however. I believe I might learn something from your messy ways."

"This is where I'm supposed to admit I would benefit by reining in my splashy emotions, and being more like you."

"Typically, yes. This would be the right time to make that admission."

Anne sniffed. The northern lights throbbed toward them, pulsed, receded.

"I can give you an opportunity to practice *reining it in,* as you say." Jane cleared her throat. "Tlingit had to be tranquillized at the dump. We examined her at the rescue facility, and she has been successfully relocated north of Wager Bay."

"What? Tlingit... How long was she anaesthetized? She was already compromised! Is she outfitted with transceivers?"

They walked back toward the motel. For the first time since they met, Jane's clipped, methodical answers to questions didn't bother Anne. *It's her nature, she can't change it. She's right, we should accept our differences.* When the neon 'Pacific Motor Inn' sign was half a block away, Gilbert's truck pulled up alongside the two women.

"Enjoying the light show? We'll see it really well from Gary and Sandra's deck. Climb in. Ian is following us with Little Ted."

Anne clambered in and slid over next to Gilbert. She held out her hand to Jane and pulled her onto the bench seat. Jane slammed the truck door.

"Why are we going to Gary and Sandra's?" Anne asked.

"The Spirit bear has returned. I guess Gary will explain when we get there. Oh, and Charlotte's in labour."

* * *

"Charlotte's at her in-laws' place in Terrace. Her water broke about seven o'clock. Walter, her husband, is going to keep me updated. They're timing her contractions, five minutes apart right now."

Anne put her hand on Gilbert's shoulder. They were all outside behind Gary and Sandra's house, on a broad wooden deck running the length of the house. Gilbert had introduced everyone. Little Ted was there too, abandoning his taxi in favour of watching the northern lights.

"Are you guys okay?" Ian asked Jane quietly, jerking his head in Anne's direction.

"We cleared a hurdle of sorts."

"So here's the deal," said Gary. His hair was disheveled, a forelock covered one eye. The buttons of his plaid jacket were done up over the prominent swell of his paunch. Sandra bobbed her head as her husband spoke, enforcing his facts with her tacit agreement.

"Our bear was seen north of here on McClintock Road, browsing on berries. The lady who spotted him noticed his paws were black, and called that new Environment Canada number for reporting oil-damaged wildlife. Those guys at the environment office know I've been flying around looking for this bear, so they gave me a call. We have a helicopter pilot prepared to transport the bear in the morning. I told 'em we got a sharpshooter to do the tranquilizing—a specialist from Churchill. That's you, right?"

Ian bowed in acknowledgement.

"Two years as an army cadet in my twenties, lots of success on the rifle range. Good deal of practice on the polar bears, lately."

"Super. Let's go inside, and have a look at the map."

The northern lights were still rippling above them, but they filed inside. Sandra poured out from a pot of tea. Little Ted slapped Gilbert's back.

"See you later, folks. I'm back to work."

"Thanks, Ted," Gilbert said. "Really, I mean it."

Gary spread out a map on the kitchen table. He jabbed a finger at a spot just outside the grid of Kitimat's streets.

"Here's the bear's approximate location. The conservation people are dropping bait here, here, and here." Gary indicated a narrowing scalene triangle. "With the bear in this approximate area, we can herd him in along this road," he drew his finger along a line parallel to the Kitimat River, "and move him within range. The helicopter can set down within twenty or thirty meters of a given spot, almost anywhere along here."

"When you say *herd him in,* what does that entail, exactly?" asked Jane.

"We walk the east and west boundaries, with noisemakers and bear spray... But we're not going to have to spray him. If this guy were aggressive, he would have attacked a few weeks ago, when he was cornered. Ian waits here," Gary tapped the map repeatedly, "at the tip of the funnel. With a bit of luck, we'll scare him out onto the road, and you'll have a good bead on him, Ian. All of us will be in radio contact, all the time. Channel three. You can pick up the handsets at the conservation office in the morning."

"Are we assuming the bear is a male?" Anne asked.

"We're drawing a conclusion based on size. Now, Sandra and I don't have any experience slinging up bears in nets. We have the wildlife net, but no one around here has used it."

"Ian and I assisted in a transport in Churchill three days ago," Jane said. "I'm confident we can safely transport this animal. Anne, is there anything we can do about the oil on his paws?"

"Plain old detergent is what the cleanup crew has been using around here. The least toxic and most effective thing, they say. I'll have a backpack with water and soap and brushes, and work quickly once we land at his new location. I'll get as much off as I can before he comes around."

"Where are we taking him?" Gilbert asked.

"The Gitga'at Conservancy, in the Great Bear Rainforest," Gary said, and Gilbert smiled.

"He might swim to the mainland again, but I doubt it. Salmon's running in Gitga'at territory now, should be bear heaven."

Gilbert and Anne dropped Jane and Ian off at their motel.

"Thank you for coming," Anne directed this at Jane.

"I'm glad we're here."

"I feel all warm and fuzzy, all of a sudden," said Ian.

"Shut up, Ian." Anne grinned.

"But what about Charlotte?" Anne asked Gilbert, as they drove back to his cabin.

"Well, what can I do? She's having her baby. I asked Gary to fly me to Terrace, once we have Moksgm'ol set up in the Gitga'at. I'll be too tired to drive. He said he would. I'll stay in Terrace for a week, likely. You can stay here, Anne. If you want to. If you can."

They didn't look at each other.

"I can't think past tomorrow," Anne said.

The Great Bear Creates the Aurora Borealis

The Great Bear created the earth, and all of the bears of the earth. She created people, and then the other creatures of the earth. As she invented her creatures, she wrote their stories in the stars. On any clear night, we can look up and read the stories of the Great Bear in the constellations.

One day, the Great Bear was walking in the sky, looking down at the earth she had created. She looked to the east, and saw a panda sow nuzzling her newborn cubs. The Great Bear saw the tender nuzzling of the cubs against their mother's soft belly, and the sow's devotion to her offspring.

Then the Great Bear looked to the west and saw a grizzly mother catching fish and feeding them to her cubs. The Great Bear could see that the grizzly mother was hungry herself and wanted to feed, yet she fed her young cubs first, and watched while they consumed the meal she had caught for them.

To the south, the Great Bear saw three black bears being threatened by a pack of wolves. One of the black bears was elderly; it certainly would not survive a wolf attack alone. The two younger bears moved to protect the older bear, blocking the wolves with their bodies. They stood on their hind legs and roared, then dropped and charged, until the wolves were dissuaded from their attack.

The Great Bear finished her survey of the compass points in the north, and there she saw a pair of one-year-old polar bears, brother and sister, playing with each other. They swatted each other, and wrestled, and rolled in the snow. When they needed to rest, they rested together, each waiting for the other to catch his or her breath before springing into play-action again.

The Great Bear saw her bears, and she expanded with irrepressible joy. Her joy came out of her in immense waves of light and colour, shimmering and spreading out over the skies. These displays of the Great Bear's joy are visible in the night sky as the northern lights, or the Aurora Borealis.

Forest near Kitimat

The sound of the wood-frame screen door banging open and closed woke Jonathan. His vision adjusting to the dimness, he watched Gilbert and Anne tiptoe past him to the little back bedroom. It felt like the middle of the night – what had they been doing? He had missed out again, and he hadn't even slept well in compensation. Inside his sleeping bag, his bear-scars itched and ached. But it wasn't his injuries keeping him awake.

He didn't want to move back in with his Vancouver roommates. They were great people, all of them, but living with four or five random people was getting old. The floors were usually an obstacle course of stale ashtrays, discarded clothes, rolling papers, and pizza crusts. Inviting a girl over meant risking at minimum disdain, if not outright revulsion. Jonathan's career counsellor at the college had advised him, *find a job in your field as soon as possible.* But jobs in environmental sustainability were pretty thin on the ground.

"The bottle depot is hiring," one of his roommates had suggested. "You know, the recycling centre. That's, like, environmental sustainability. Right?"

He heard Gilbert and Anne talking to each other, a low and loving exchange. He imagined them spooning, murmuring endearments, snuggling up to each other's naked bodies...

Jonathan slept fitfully until dawn, waking every quarter hour to change his position on the couch. Frustrated, he rolled over, wincing as the couch pinched his bruised leg. Leaning forward, he pushed himself upright, yawning. He was tired of waiting around, playing Cinderella in this cabin. He decided to limp to the main spill cleanup volunteer tent. It wasn't far away, he and Gilbert had passed it on their way home with the pizza. He could be there in half an hour. He got dressed, made himself two jam sandwiches, and snuck outside, careful not to wake Anne and Gilbert. He didn't leave them a note.

Outside the air was thick and damp. Thin banks of fog drifted in from the ocean. A spiky coating of hoar frost on the grass and fallen leaves gave the morning a freshly minted feeling, like he was the first person to see the world that day. He was suspicious of shiny patches of pavement, which were probably icy as hell. A fall would compound his misery.

He got to the volunteer tent an hour before anyone else arrived. A convenience store across the street sold him a cup of thin, watery coffee. He drank it from the styrofoam cup it came in, trying not to think about the landfill where the cup would end up. At last the volunteer coordinators arrived. When he explained his physical limitations, they assigned him the job of Traffic Control and Perimeter Security Guard. He was tasked with sitting in a lawn chair beside a barrier of orange traffic cones. Elba Energy trucks were allowed past his checkpoint, as were police and emergency vehicles, oil pump trucks, and City of Kitimat municipal vehicles. He was supposed to turn away all other traffic.

The first two hours of his shift, Jonathan napped. When he woke up, fog that when he fell asleep had hidden the trees and mountains from him, had evaporated. He blinked, unsure of where he was, and what he was doing there. A shiny black SUV drove up to the row of cones. He stood with difficulty, his legs numb from resting on the aluminum chair frame.

"Sorry, this road's closed. You can turn around half a kilometre away, up at the next intersection."

And then Jonathan waited, alone on a muddy road on the outskirts of Kitimat, without seeing another vehicle, for two hours. He attributed rustling in the trees to squirrels and birds, then it began to unnerve him. He pressed the 'talk' button on his portable radio phone. A static-broken voice answered, *Central site here, over.* He pressed the 'talk' button again.

"Nothing, pressed it by mistake. Sorry."

The person on the other end clicked their button in acknowledgement, kind of huffily, Jonathan thought. Then the road was quiet again. He should have brought a book. Still, this was better than spending another day hanging around Gilbert's cabin, peeling carrots.

He settled back into the folding lawn chair, a cheap and flawed piece of furniture that was developing a warp in one leg from his attempts to make it into a recliner. Overhead, the sky was boiling. Grey shreds of storm clouds surfed by, hanging low under patches of white light. The surrounding mountainsides were covered mainly with conifers, but here and there bursts of yellow, orange, and red deciduous trees flared like matches.

Clouds moved in and hid the mountains again. The roadside trees seemed to loom over him, and a misty, thin rain began to fall. The chair was cutting off the circulation in his legs, so Jonathan got up and limped up and down the road, peering into the forest. He saw a tree in there, a cedar. The trunk must have been two meters wide at the base. A branch cracked, and he almost fell over retreating to his lawn chair which, now that he thought about it, wasn't much of a defensive weapon.

Jonathan took a deep breath, held it, and exhaled slowly. The petroleum smell wasn't noticeable here. Maybe the forest was filtering it out, or maybe the oil molecules had dissipated. The air was clean, invigorating. It smelled like mud, ocean, and oxygen, with spicy undertones of bark, spruce needles, and sap. If he could bottle it, reproduce that smell somehow, he'd be rich. He remembered that people had tried to make pine-scented sprays and deodorizers, and these things always smelled like a chemical soup.

It began to rain harder, lightly but steadily. He squinted down the road beyond his makeshift barrier. There was something moving in the roadside shrubbery. He saw a flash of something blonde. It was an animal, judging by its height. Probably someone's golden retriever, off leash. A head emerged from the tall grass in the ditch, and then a bear sauntered, slowly and leisurely, onto the road. Jonathan stood up in alarm, toppling his lawn chair.

"No way," he breathed.

What were the chances? Was he some kind of bear magnet? At least this one was a Spirit bear, a kind of black bear, and not a grizzly. But still – another bear! He wouldn't be attacked again, he told himself, his heart slamming into his ribs, his breathing shallow. The chances were infinitely small. It would see him, and be afraid of him, and go back in the forest – wouldn't it? Through his fear, Jonathan marvelled at the hue of the bear's fur, a rich yellow-gold. It stood placidly in the centre of the dirt road, which ran parallel to the river.

The bridge to downtown wasn't far away. Where were all the cars he was supposed to be rerouting? If he squinted, Jonathan could see a building through the trees, the backside of a concrete strip mall. Pricking up his ears, he heard the swoosh of cars and trucks on wet roads. He was close to people and help, but was he close enough? When they had dropped him off that morning, civilization had seemed close by. But if that bear were to charge him...

The seconds dragged on, and still the bear stayed on the road. It swung its head casually in his direction, then the other way. The rain fell harder, muffling the city sounds. Jonathan didn't know whether to act naturally, or turn and walk away as quickly as his bear-inflicted injuries would allow. He thought about his lunch, a jelly sandwich and two apples, wrapped in a plastic bag and zipped into his nylon backpack.

Between Jonathan and the bear another human being emerged, slow and stealthy, from the thick roadside foliage. He was exceptionally tall, and he had a gun, some sort of rifle. Jonathan didn't know anything about guns, but it looked like the kind of gun you would use to kill a bear. *What the hell?* The hunter eased his way expertly along the treeline, staying partly camouflaged by the roadside shrubs. He was focused on the bear, and didn't notice Jonathan. He wore khaki pants, a plaid shirt, and an orange vest. With a smooth, fluid movement, he swung the weapon into his arms, and aimed it at the bear.

You can't shoot a goddamn Spirit bear! Jonathan wanted to scream. But what if his shout scared the bear, and it turned, and charged him? Bears had notoriously poor eyesight, didn't they? And what if this bonehead, this Spirit bear hunter, blasted off a lousy shot, injuring the bear, but not killing it? Frozen, petrified, Jonathan watched the hunter approach the bear. Then two more people came out of the forest, on the far side of the bear! They were women, he saw, in hiking clothes and orange vests. The shooter saw them, and they saw the shooter. The women waved at the hunter, and he nodded back at them.

My God, thought Jonathan, *they flushed it out for him. These people are sick, they're criminals!*

In a moment of blinding brilliance, Jonathan knew what he should do. He could jump-start his career, and salvage his reputation. He could go home to Vancouver with a proud feather in his environmental sustainability cap. Headlines formed in his mind, *Volunteer Thwarts Poachers, Hero Environmental Activist Saves Spirit Bear.*

Jonathan reached down, carefully picked up the lawn chair with both hands, and collapsed it. He choked up on the folded legs of the chair, testing the heft of his baseball-bat shaped weapon. He crept up behind the shooter, walking heel-to-toe, the steady patter of rain muffling his approach. The women didn't see him coming. They were intent on the bear.

He was right behind the hunter, lawn chair raised, muscles tensed, when one of the women turned around. It was Anne, and his brain recognized her, but his nerve endings were committed and his purpose was clear.

"*No, don't!*" Anne shrieked.

Jonathan swung. The hunter's gun made a muted popping sound, and a fraction of a second later, Jonathan's lawn chair connected with the side of the hunter's head.

The bear loped into the forest. Ian sank to one knee, howling.

"Sweet withering Christ, you hit me!"

Ian pivoted on his bent knee to face his attacker, his face twisted in agony. Jonathan, bewildered, stood dripping in the rain, his weapon still aloft.

"With a *lawn* chair – you hit me with a *lawn* chair!"

The smack had broken the chair; one leg hung down askew. Anne and the other woman took off into the forest, following the bear. Just before she disappeared into the tree line, Anne pulled a two-way radio from a holster on her chest and barked something urgent into it. A wretched suspicion that he may have acted too quickly stole over Jonathan.

"Easy now," Ian said warily, his words blurred by the pain in his jaw. "Put down the chair, and step away from it, okay? Step *away* from the chair. Yes, that's right."

Jonathan released his grip, let the lawn chair fall into the mud, and took two lurching steps backward. Ian sat down heavily in the road, holding his head between his hands.

"That *really* hurt! I'm going to have one hell of a bruise. Is there a good reason why I shouldn't deck you right now? Who *are* you, anyway?"

"You can't shoot a Spirit bear. It isn't right."

"Oh, boy. Wow. Um, this is a dart gun, son. It shoots a hypodermic needle charged with an anaesthetic. That bear has been compromised by the oil spill, and we're relocating it. Listen!"

The *whump whump whump* of a helicopter was closing in. They both scanned the sky, and abruptly the helicopter was right above them, a long rope dangling underneath it. It hovered over a spot some two hundred meters away. The rope hung down into the trees.

The rhythmic beating of the helicopter's rotors drowned out everything. The treetops under the helicopter splayed out in unnatural directions, then the aircraft flew away, the rope underneath it shorter than it had been.

"So, you're *relocating* that bear!" Jonathan shouted.

Ian didn't answer. The helicopter returned, hovered over the same spot as before, then rose vertically, revealing a bundle of creamy fur suspended below it in a red net. The helicopter tilted, then followed the river, heading west toward the Douglas Channel and the Pacific Ocean.

Ian and Jonathan watched until the helicopter was a tiny speck in grey mist, its rotor beats faint. Rain continued to hiss on the road and in the forest. Chipmunks were chattering close by. Jonathan was miserable.

"Wow, man. I am so incredibly sorry. I just keep screwing up over and over again up here. Please don't, like, charge me with assault. I really thought you were going to kill that bear."

Ian, still seated on the ground, regarded the dejected young man standing above him. The poor kid's shoulders had collapsed, his head hung down. He had a strangely delicate stance, fragile, as though he were made of glass.

"What's your story, kid?" asked Ian.

Jonathan closed his eyes. He wanted the rain to wash him away.

"Okay, you don't have to tell me. But I think I need a hospital. Do you know where it is? I think my jaw might be broken."

"Kitimat Health Centre. I know the way."

"Well, lead on," said Ian. "You do the talking. My mouth hurts."

Ian took the hand Jonathan held out. Jonathan pulled Ian upright, and radioed the volunteer centre to tell them he was abandoning his post. They walked over the bridge to town in the rain, Jonathan glumly relating the story of the grizzly bear attack.

"You are the luckiest—"

"I know, I know! But that's where the luck ends, man. I came up here to camp, meet other environmentalists, schmooze with them, and maybe talk my way into a job. Instead I've got a shredded tent, shredded legs, and a shredded ego. Shreds, that's what I've got."

Moksgm'ol

There is thirst, and there is nothing to be done but find water to drink. The creeks run low and dry after the hot-sun time, the river calls to Moksgm'ol. Scant berries, the hapless doe I took two nights ago—they have not slaked my great hunger, and so again Moksgm'ol must go to the river. The river, fat with fish, beckons me. Impure foulness of men stains my paws, but I must descend to eat and drink. Moksgm'ol must approach the foul domain of man once more.

I pick a cautious route, thick of bush and tall of grass. These stains upon my paws are an indelible evil. The balance between man and bear has been tipped. Where once men kept to their villages, respecting the domain of Moksgm'ol, now they infiltrate my kingdom, and do not act afraid. Men have hemmed in the river that brings plenty; they have bordered it with their grey ways of death. Men venture into mountain and meadow, where before they never dared. Easily, Moksgm'ol eludes them, and keeps forest and fern between bear and man. Moksgm'ol will fill his belly and quench his great thirst, and retreat once more to parts untainted by men.

Here, the lowlands. I skirt a meadow of tall, brown grass. My creamy fur blends in with the thick fronds. The shrubs here are still heavy with fruit, and I soften the urgency of my hunger. A fine rain falls, refreshing my body, but intensifying my thirst. My nose leads me to some abandoned apples, redolent of men. Desperate, I eat them anyway. I come to the place where a grey way bisects the wilderness. I must cross it to reach the river. Rain-hushed quiet prevails. Moksgm'ol proceeds onto the grey way. I survey my surroundings.

Man. A man is there, some distance from me. Is it a trap, a trick? I do not venture forward to the river, nor do I return from whence I came. I am still and stately. I am Moksgm'ol!

As I stand my ground, another man emerges onto the grey way. He is some distance from me. I stand, proud —

Pain! Ah, pain in my side, pain, I run, crash, and run from man's terrible trick. I run into the fern forest, the thickest undergrowth I run from pain—ah, the pain!

Ah.

This is some new trick—some trick of time. All things are slowing. All things are slowing down. Now the edge of trees blurs, the ground rushes up to meet Moksgm'ol' crashing down. Man makes strange sounds. A Man too close.

I stop and sleep? Sleep, Man beside Moksgm'ol?

Man makes sounds. I sleep.

Forest near Kitimat

Gilbert waited in the forest, thinking about Charlotte and remembering Clara in the throes of childbirth, her sweat-drenched hair, her body wracked with contractions, her eyes turned inward, moving through agony. He imagined his new grandchild drawing a first breath in the world. He prayed to the Creator to keep Charlotte and her baby safe, and he talked to Clara in his mind. *Charlotte's having a little brother or sister for Jack. She's with Walter's family. I will go to her once the bear is safe.*

There was a fine, misty rain. He heard it up in the canopy, but few drops reached him on the fallen log where he sat, on a cushion of springy yellow-green moss. It was a nurse log, a fallen tree feeding dozens of small, spindly seedlings along her length. He ran a finger along the soft, tender needles of a young Sitka spruce.

Anne would make a wonderful mother. She would be like Clara had been, on the floor playing dolls or cars, an immersed participant in her children's imaginary worlds. She would take her babies out in the yard and in the forest, discover tiny winged insects and giant, ancient cedars.

Anne will want babies, he thought, and I'm fifty-one this year, my own children are having children. Was it possible, was it advisable, should he start another family?

The bleeping of his two-way radio interrupted his thoughts. It was Anne's voice, broken and distorted.

"He's hit, headed toward you, do you copy?"

"Copy that."

He stood and scanned the forest, and right away he found the bear's blonde head, rising and falling, running in his direction. Gilbert made himself small, invisible, not a threat. The bear halted, faltered, turned his great head, and chewed ferociously at his own flank, then charged again toward the river, and stopped once more to bite at the foreign object embedded in his skin. When Moksgm'ol pressed forward again, he was slower, confused. The bear had begun his ungainly slide into unconsciousness.

It didn't take long. Gilbert watched the bear stagger, swoon and collapse. It was gut-wrenching, as if the animal had died. There was no one else in sight, which wasn't the plan. Three or four members of the team should have been close when Moksgm'ol went down. What was holding them up? He wouldn't be able to net the bear by himself. At least the bear had gone down in a logistically good location, a relatively open patch of second-growth forest.

"Bear down, mark my location." Gilbert said into his radio. They were prepared to use GPS to find each other, but as the sound of helicopter rotors shuddered through the trees, Anne and Jane showed up, crashing through the underbrush, rain-soaked and muddy.

Gilbert knelt down beside the bear. The animal's paws were blackened, ragged from chewing and licking. Moksgm'ol's eyes weren't yet closed; they were red-rimmed, pupils rolling, wild with fear and confusion. Surprising himself, Gilbert started singing, a traditional song his grandmother had loved. The helicopter was loud overhead, but he sang anyway. Jane dropped to her knees beside the bear, acknowledging

Gilbert with a curt bob of her head. He kept singing. The bear's eyes closed at last.

Anne plunged her hand into fur, checking the animal's pulse. She picked up a paw and put it in her lap, frowning. A thick rope snaked out of the belly of the helicopter, weighted down by the transport net. Gilbert got up and lunged for the rope, unclipped the heavy, bulky net, and dragged it beside the bear. Gary and Sandra arrived, panting and sweating.

"Where's Ian?" Gary shouted.

"Long story!" Anne said. "He won't make it in time."

Helicopter rotors hammered the air. The pilot flew to the road and landed. In the forest, the five remaining members of the team rolled Moksgm'ol onto the spread-out net. Once the bear was centred in the net, Gilbert, Anne and Jane sprinted to the road and got in the helicopter, which then once again rose and hovered over the forest. Gary and Sandra hooked the net to the rope hanging from the helicopter. The mechanical bird rose straight up, rotated to face southwest, and flew away.

Moksgm'ol and the Great Bear

The Great Bear has called me to her. I walk among the stars. There are other creatures here with me, though I cannot see them clearly. Some unscrupulous contrivance of man has defeated me, Moksgm'ol, the White Bear of the West. I walked unhindered, feared and respected, through the rocky majesty of my homeland. In ages past, I made magic in the forest at the behest of one greater than me, and now I have passed on to her Sky World.

She appears to me. She is One-bear. She is Every-bear. I bow my head, and bend my forelegs. I prostrate myself before her. I am humbled by She who created us all.

After a time, I dare to raise my eyes, and behold her once more. Fear, dismay! There is a man with her. He is a male, and he is naked. He stands beside her, insignificant in her presence, yet familiar enough to touch her, immerse a hand in her iridescent fur. My teeth long to bite, my claws long to shred, and remove the threat of this man—who helped bring about my untimely fate.

But inside Moksgm'ol there is a sound, and the instinct to attack the man dwindles. The sound repeats, hey ah ya wey, hey ah ya wey. It is strangely calming. The Great Bear sways with the sound, and I find that I move with the sound also.

The stars around the Great Bear and the man become brighter and brighter, until I can no longer make out shapes. Everything is swallowed in a white glare. The sound continues, hey ah ya wey. Moksgm'ol dreams in a deep sleep, at peace.

Kitimat

Walter and Jack dropped off Charlotte and the baby at the cabin in Kitimat. Father and son were going shopping, and letting mother and newborn rest. Gilbert took the soft white flannel bundle in his arms, round brown eyes, jagged shock of jet-black hair. Two perfect, miniature hands punched the air, clenching and flexing. Charlotte sank onto the couch beside Jonathan's bedroll and yawned.

"What time was she born?" Anne hovered at Gilbert's elbow.

"Eleven in the morning. Dad, you and Gary must have been in the air right then. I can't believe you guessed her name. I still think Walter told you."

"Nope." Gilbert held his granddaughter closer to him. "Aurora. Gosh, Charlotte, she's so beautiful."

"How is that bear?" Charlotte asked.

"The transceiver shows lots of normal, vigorous movement and activity," said Anne. "I think he loves his new home."

"So, are you going back to Churchill now?"

Anne glanced at Gilbert. He was engrossed with the warm little human in his arms. They hadn't decided what, if anything, to say to Max and Charlotte about their romance.

"My plans are up in the air. There's a lot of desk-work I can do from here, and frankly I'm still enjoying the break from Churchill. Ian and Jane are there, they can keep things rolling without me for awhile."

Gilbert looked up from Aurora.

"I didn't see Ian before he left – how was his face?"

"Colourful," Anne smiled. "Speaking of Ian's face, where's Slugger?"

"He's at work." Gilbert passed his granddaughter to Anne, whose expression softened. She sat down beside Charlotte on the couch.

"Work? I thought the oil spill clean up was quote-unquote finished." Charlotte adjusted her weight on the couch, wincing.

Anne cooed at Aurora, and offered a finger for the baby to grasp in her fist.

"Jonathan got a job with Elba Energy," Gilbert said.

"What, really? What kind of job?" Anne asked. The baby started fussing. Anne placed Aurora in her mother's arms.

Gilbert shrugged.

"Impact studies, he said, and a little liaising with the media. Don't worry Anne, he's not going to live with us. Little Ted's letting him crash at his place until Jonathan gets his first paycheque."

"With *us?* When you say it like that, Dad, it sounds like you and Anne are an item," said Charlotte.

"But – how can Jonathan work for an oil company?" Anne frowned.

Gilbert walked over to the kitchen and put the kettle on the stove, talking over his shoulder.

"The world doesn't change overnight. Now, more than ever, companies like Elba Energy need people like Jonathan. If they had been employing some decent environmental sustainability assessors prior to building the pipeline, they probably wouldn't be getting slapped with a multimillion-dollar cleanup bill right now, and countless property damage lawsuits."

"But Elba Energy is just going to find the cheapest way to put a Band-Aid on this spill, and keep selling crude oil overseas! And Jonathan's going to help them spin it? Oh, I'm so disappointed in him."

Nursing the baby, Charlotte interrupted.

"A minute ago, it totally sounded like you two have hooked up."

"Change is hard for humanity," said Gilbert, dropping two tea bags into a cracked ceramic teapot. "It's like...birth. Think about it this way – what if Charlotte's body is the planet?"

"I resent that. I gained a little extra weight during this pregnancy, but nothing—*nothing* —compared to how much I gained with Jack."

Gilbert laughed.

"You're beautiful Charlotte, you're the world. Inside you is humanity, gestating, slowly growing, gaining knowledge and experience. But ultimately none of that growth is going to amount to anything, unless we push out of the comfortable body we're inside, out into the scary unknown. And getting out won't be easy. It's going to hurt."

"You can say that again," Charlotte sighed. "But moving along from grizzly boy's employment status, are you guys, you know..?"

* * *

In the middle of October, the first snow fell in Kitimat. Gilbert smelled and felt it before he saw it, clean and fresh, cooling the air. The snow scrubbed the atmosphere on its descent, leaf and earth and grass smells buried in pure white crystals. He found himself wondering where his wool socks were. He was still under the covers, curled up with Anne. She was behind him, sleeping soundly, her breasts snugged up to his back, one smooth arm draped over his hip bone. Her nose whistled a little on each of her inhalations.

The bedroom window was cracked a centimetre, and muted traffic sounds filtered in from outside, tires spinning on unploughed distant streets. The snowy hush was broken by the sound of a vehicle approaching, sliding, and stopping in front of the cabin. Gilbert heard the metallic creak-and-slam of a truck door opening and closing, and he thought he knew whose truck it was. He heard footsteps on the front porch stairs, and a light tapping on the cabin door. Gingerly, he lifted Anne's arm, and slid out from underneath her.

"I love you," she murmured.

"I know."

He donned the previous day's jeans and a plaid shirt, and found his socks.

It was Max. Gilbert let him in, and turned to make coffee. Max kicked the snow off his boots, shook his arms out of a blue down-filled *Kitimat Tire Shop* jacket, and padded to the kitchen table. The way he sat there expectantly, anticipating being served, made time slide sideways for Gilbert. It was the same table where Max had eaten his whole life, until recently. There he was, an awkward teenager slouching in his chair, a restless young boy jiggling his knees, and a round and red-cheeked squalling baby.

Neither of them spoke until the coffee was ready, and Gilbert sat down.

"Aurora looks like Mom."

Gilbert nodded in agreement. Privately he didn't think his granddaughter looked like anyone yet, but he was glad that Max saw Clara in Aurora.

"You have a girlfriend," Max said.

“Her name is Anne.” Gilbert motioned briefly at his bedroom door, acknowledging her presence.

“Oh. Well, that’s cool.”

Max tossed this out offhand, but Gilbert knew he meant it, and was relieved his son didn’t think he and Anne were insulting Clara’s memory.

“Charlotte says it makes her sad, but she’s okay with it.”

Max didn’t reply. He sipped his coffee, took his cell phone out of his pocket and checked it, scrolling through a few pages before he spoke again.

“Guess I was wrong about a spill never happening.”

There was nothing to say. Gilbert sipped his coffee. Max fiddled with his phone.

“Business must have picked up at the tire shop, though?”

“Yeah, sure. The Elba Energy trucks are getting their winters on today. It’s going to be a really busy one.”

A snowplow drove by outside, its metal blade scraping the asphalt and its engine roaring. They both watched the front door until the noise faded away.

“The fact is, I don’t want to work at the tire shop for the rest of my life. I never told you this, but I always kind of wanted to be a fishing guide.”

“So what’s stopping you? You’d be a great fishing guide.”

A slide show of fishing trips with Max played in Gilbert’s head. Summers in their aluminum boat with an outboard motor, walking down to the river with their rods after school, deep-sea expeditions for halibut from Prince Rupert. When Max was fishing he was quiet and patient. He was friendly enough to work with the public, and stern enough to tell greedy tourists that they were over their catch limit.

“Yeah, well, who wants to fish around here *now?*” said Max bitterly. “I didn’t think it was going to happen, I thought they had it figured out, so this wouldn't happen. I guess I understand now, why you were so against it. The whole time, I thought you were doing it for Mom."

They drank their coffee. Gilbert got up and fed the wood stove another small log. The fire crackled and spat.

"Good to see you, Dad. I've gotta go to work."

Max tipped his mug back and gulped down the rest of his coffee. At the front door, he put a hand on the wall to steady himself while he pushed his feet, in thick woollen socks, into his snow boots. He zipped up his jacket.

Gilbert followed Max to the door. They hugged, Max pulling away quickly.

"I'll stop by again soon. To meet Anne."

"I'd like that."

Gilbert watched Max get into his truck and drive away. He watched until the truck's taillights disappeared around the corner. Then everything was snow-covered and quiet once more.

TLINGIT

The nightmare of man-things is over. Ice everywhere. Everywhere, there is ice. The World of the Bear is everywhere. My stomach is shrieking, but already I see Seal slither underneath the ice. I push the ice with my paws and it is heavy, thick. Thick heavy ice holds Tlingit.

I ask the Great Bear for patience, and stand where seal soon will come. It is cold! O perfect coldness, all around me. A light snow dusts my fur. Lick and lick, it is so good—perfect, whiteness to the edges. White and ice and cold.

It happens quickly. Seal pops up and out of the water, slides and slips onto ice. Seal never sees the white bear of winter. With merciful speed I bite, where seal's head meets seal's body. Spray of red blood on white snow. Thank you, seal, for your life. Thank you, seal, for the gift of your life, to strengthen my life. Thank Great Bear for whiteness everywhere.

I devour this animal—slash, rip, gulp—and walk again and wait for seal, and again seal comes, and again Tlingit eats flesh. Flesh of two seals. My belly is full, for the first time since K'ytuk was inside me. Hunger recedes.

A freezing north wind blows. O north wind, your sting and bite sustain me. Sharp needles of a snowstorm blow, white curtains, everywhere. O K'ytuk, here, in this frozen place of white bears, you could have lived. K'ytuk, I will always remember you.

Moksgm'ol

I wake, and there is the sound of surf crashing onto rocks, and the distant screaming of gulls. My body is heavy; I have been sleeping a long time. I stand, raise my head, open my senses. The air is pure with unadulterated clean smells of forest, ocean, and fern. I detect late fall berries, a hint of fresh fish, and moist earth, sweet layers of leaves. My nostrils quiver in delight. I listen, rotating my ears and turning my head. I can hear Squirrel scrabbling on bark, scampering from branch to branch. Ah – the heavier hoof-beats of Deer! My mouth waters. Moksgm'ol, the great hunter, shall feast before the day is done.

What is this place? My senses tell a delightful story, a story of absences. The strange stench of recent days is gone. A small remnant clings to a few tainted hairs of my paws. Still, the stink is faint. My paws, magically, are clean. I inhale natural perfumes of the earth. Perhaps the Great Bear has answered my prayers!

I do not recognize this stream, or these rocks. I do not recognize this shore or these trees. I have woken in an unfamiliar paradise. Or perhaps I am dreaming, and will wake once more to men and their machines? I think not. I dreamed I soared above the trees and rivers, like Eagle. In the dream there was a strange sound, and I was touched by hands of men.

Impossible! I stretch my limbs and yawn. Yes, I am Moksgm'ol, the Spirit Bear, returned to my kingdom!

The Great Bear Welcomes Yukuai

The bright daylight of the sky above my enclosure fades. Gradually, I am immersed in total darkness. The great weight of my earthly form—four heavy black limbs, white barrel-body—descends from me. It sinks beneath, and drifts away. The chatter of human voices, which has plagued me for so long, is silenced at last. I am suspended in a dream of lightless, weightless peace.

The dream goes on without my body. I am aware. Nothingness, the absence of all stimuli, is intensely pleasurable. If this is all there is—if this sensation extends into limitless time—then I should be a grateful bear.

At an indeterminate moment, there is change. Light comes, little by little, illuminating my surroundings. It is sunlight, and it dapples a clearing of tall, swaying, blue-green cylinders. I am in a forest of towering wet green stalks. There are rich earth-smells, and the air is full of crisp chlorophyll. They must be hollow, these softly swaying stalks. Low, beautiful musical tones sound out when two of them touch. I am in some earthly place, yet the comfort of weightlessness remains. I am aware of the parameters of what used to be my body.

A Bear, larger than me, appears beside me. I am calm, but I cannot make out where this other Bear begins, and where She ends. She thinks, and her thoughts are known to me—not between the soft black tufts that used to be my ears, but in my core.

The bamboo groves of your youth, Yukuai—you didn't dream them, after all. I thought you would want to see them again, before we go onward.

The heart of this place is the heart of me. It swells up and fills me with green fibres and clear water. The bamboo grove becomes more tangible, running water over smooth stones, and sparkling dew droplets on sweet blue-green leaves. It is right to be reunited with this place, but there is also terrible sadness—a sombre understanding, and the knowledge of what-might-have-been.

Yukuai. Long you have suffered. Your earthly journey has been a vexatious, arduous one.

In a flash, I compress pain, fire, flames, screams, cold, hunger, confinement, illness, mockery, fear, loneliness, and boredom. I make all this into a ball of anguish and I push this ball toward the Bear beside me.

Yes, all this is your truth, Yukuai. There is no might-have-been. There is only what is, and what was.

Tear-stars sparkle in the Great Bear's eyes.

Linger here in this place, and be healed.

Time ceases to be quantifiable. Among the tuneful movement of tall bamboo, I simply am. I exist here in perfect comfort, stripped of all biology, never hungry or cold or stricken by any physical sensations. Small black butterflies make their erratic way amongst the plants. Little white bellflowers in the undergrowth emit a soothing perfume. An ever-present sun warms the imaginary fur of my back. A never-ending breeze cools and soothes a body that doesn't exist. Without irony or falsehood, I become that for which I was named. I am Happy.

Either a million years or mere moments pass. It doesn't matter. The knowledge of this perfect bamboo grove is a balm that heals all the sores of concrete cages, and the welts of the firestorm. It eases, without erasing, the years of my earthly existence.

The Great Bear comes again. She is beside me, and I know a peace that living beings cannot know.

Come, Yukuai. Walk with me among the stars.

Proof

Made in the USA
Charleston, SC
20 December 2016